TRIAL RUN

Scott Lavin looked at Joe and said, "How would you like to drive this baby?"

Joe's mouth dropped open. He was actually getting a chance to drive the ultimate racing machine—a Formula One car.

Joe stepped into the cockpit and slid down into the seat. "Okay," he said eagerly. "Here goes nothing."

As Joe carefully put the car in gear and drove toward the race course, Scott turned to Frank and said, "He's pretty good. Most guys stall out the first time they get behind the wheel."

"Joe's a fast learner," Frank replied. Then he heard a shout rise up from the small cluster of spectators.

A black cloud began to billow over the race course. The trail of acrid smoke led down to a burning vehicle.

Horror crept up on Frank as he slowly realized it was Scott's car and Joe was still in it!

Books in THE HARDY BOYS CASEFILES® Series

Available from ARCHWAY Paperbacks

COLLISION COURSE

FRANKLIN W. DIXON

AN ARCHWAY PAPERBACK
Published by POCKET BOOKS
New York   London   Toronto   Sydney   Tokyo   Singapore

AN ARCHWAY PAPERBACK *Original*

An Archway Paperback published by
POCKET BOOKS, a division of Simon & Schuster Inc.
1230 Avenue of the Americas, New York, NY 10020

ISBN: 0-671-74666-9

First Archway Paperback printing November 1989

10 9 8 7 6 5 4 3

THE HARDY BOYS, AN ARCHWAY PAPERBACK
and colophon are registered trademarks of Simon & Schuster Inc.

THE HARDY BOYS CASEFILES is a trademark of
Simon & Schuster Inc.

Printed in the U.S.A.

IL 7+

Chapter

1

"ISN'T SHE BEAUTIFUL?" Seventeen-year-old Joe Hardy said, slipping his mirrored aviator sunglasses on top of his head.

His older brother, Frank, turned to see which girl had grabbed Joe's attention. But of course he realized in the next second that Joe meant the bright yellow-and-red machine gleaming in the sun before them.

The reflected light from its sleek body glinted in their eyes, and Joe absently pulled his sunglasses down over his blue eyes as he approached the car.

The term *car* hardly described the automobile the boys were looking at—it was more like a fighter jet on wheels, with wings in the front and back, and air intakes like airplane engines attached to each side of the bullet-shaped body.

"It looks like it could take off and fly, doesn't it?" Joe turned to greet Scott Lavin, the speaker and owner-driver of the race car. Scott was a few inches shorter than Joe and several years older. His racing jumpsuit—and protective gear underneath it—padded out his wiry frame. His hair was light brown, cut short on the top, but long in the back. At twenty-four Scott was young for his profession, but the deep creases around his green eyes made him look older.

"It sure does." Joe grinned. They both knew the car was designed to do just the opposite: it would hug the ground at high speeds and in tight turns.

"It seems so *small* for a race car," Joe added. "Look, the top of the roll bar doesn't even reach my waist."

"Well, it has to be built low to the ground," Scott noted, "and it is a tight fit in the cockpit. The whole thing's pretty compact. But the engine can crank over six hundred horsepower, and I've gotten her over two hundred miles per hour on the straightaways."

His teeth flashed in a wide grin. "Formula One Grand Prix race cars aren't very much like those stock cars that chase each other around in a circle."

"This baby's a whole different breed." Joe ran a hand along the side of the speed machine. He thought it was just about the most beautiful thing he'd ever seen.

2

"It's been a long time coming," Scott reminded him. Three years earlier, when Joe was only fourteen, Scott had been organizing and racing in amateur road rallies in Bayport. Now he had returned to his hometown with his own Formula One racing team.

"We had some good times with that old Porsche, didn't we, Joe?" Scott went on. "You may have been too young to drive it, but you sure weren't too young to take the engine apart and put it back together again."

"Not many people would have given me the chance at that age." Joe smiled at the memory. "But you accepted me without a second thought. My favorite part was when we'd road test it on the rally course that you mapped out."

"Ah, yes!" Scott chuckled. "The old Bayport Road Rally. I remember it well."

The business people of Bayport remembered the road rallies, too. Scott's careful planning and attention to detail had created a popular local event that had brought money into the city. The city council, always looking for ways to bring in *more* money, decided to expand on Scott Lavin's idea. This year they had hired a slick racing promoter named Russell Arno to organize a Formula One Grand Prix race in Bayport.

"Well, I'm not too young to drive now," Joe said, bringing his mind back to the present. "And I sure would like a chance to give this baby a spin."

"It takes more than a driver's license to handle one of these." Scott looked with pride at the car he had built himself. "But maybe you'll get your chance."

While Joe talked cars with Scott, Frank scanned the crowed, shielding his brown eyes against the sun. "There sure are a lot of people here—mostly out-of-town reporters," he said.

"Maybe we should hire a promoter like this Arno character," Joe said, flashing his brother a smile.

Frank laughed. "Yeah, our last case, *Blood Money,* should have been good for a series of comic books. All those mobsters falling over one another, trying to grab that inheritance—and Dad caught in the middle!"

Their father, Fenton Hardy, was a private investigator and former police detective. His name wound up on a hit list when a dying gangster left a fortune to his enemies. Frank and Joe had been forced to risk their own lives to protect their father from greedy mobsters.

"You'd probably feel more at home investigating Russell Arno than making a deal with him," Scott said. "He's got some kind of deal going now with Angus McCoy. I don't like the guy, but he sure knows how to pull in the racing fans."

"Angus is the former world champion Grand Prix driver," Joe added for Frank's benefit.

"McCoy is a crowd pleaser. That's why all the reporters are here. The race is still three days

away, but they all turned up for McCoy's official qualifying lap around the course."

Scott shrugged. "The time trials are important because the driver with the best time gets the best starting position. But the rest of us aren't 'noteworthy'—not when the press can cover Angus McCoy's thrilling race against the clock."

"He was the best in his day," Joe said, catching the bitterness in Scott's words. "But he's past his prime now."

"He still may be the best in this crowd." Scott stared at the assorted drivers, reporters, photographers, and race officials who were gathered for McCoy's time trial. "Everybody thinks he'll have the best lap time."

Joe saw McCoy standing next to Arno, both men surrounded by reporters. Like Scott, the lines around the champion's eyes made it hard to judge his age, and his wavy red hair and fair skin made him look like a big kid. But Joe could tell by McCoy's piercing gray eyes that he was no innocent kid.

As if sensing Joe's gaze, McCoy turned his eyes toward Joe and stared. Joe could almost feel the driver's confidence. He pulled his eyes away and put a hand on Scott's shoulder. "He'll have to be pretty fast if he wants to beat your time, Scott. Your average speed was almost one seventy!"

"Ya," came a fourth voice, with a slight German accent. "He even beat me. But I expect to do better tomorrow."

Scott turned to greet the newcomer. "Reinhart! Good to see you. Joe and Frank Hardy, meet Reinhart Voss. Reinhart is the number-two driver for the McCoy racing team."

"How many cars does McCoy have?" Frank asked.

"We used to have three," Voss said. "But times have been hard, and now we have only two. Let's hope nothing happens to McCoy's car today—or else he will end up driving mine and I will have nothing."

"That's what happens when you're number two," Scott said, laughing. "I don't have that problem. Of course, I also don't have a second car either. So if something happens to my car, I'll be sitting in the grandstand with you!"

Joe looked back in the direction of McCoy and Arno. McCoy had worn his fireproof racing suit to the press conference and was now pulling on his crash helmet as he walked to his car. Completely covered in protective gear, anybody or any*thing* could have been inside that outfit, Joe observed. Even with the helmet visor up, the driver's identity was a mystery. In fact, Joe thought that the fire retardant face mask—resembling a ski mask with two large oval holes for the eyes—made the guy look like an alien from an old sci-fi movie.

"Can we meet McCoy?" Joe suddenly asked Voss.

"Ya, sure. Come. I will take you to him."

But as the group of four moved toward the center of the crowd they were intercepted by Russell Arno. "Well, if it isn't Reinhart Voss and Scott Lavin, two of my favorite drivers. Having a good time?"

"We were just going to introduce my friends, Frank and Joe Hardy, to Angus," Scott replied curtly.

"The Hardy brothers? You boys have made quite a name for yourselves in Bayport."

Frank looked at Arno curiously. The promoter looked as if he were a middle-aged banker. His hair was thinning on top, and he was a little overweight—but his tailored suit was cut beautifully and made him look thinner.

"Where did you hear that?" Frank asked.

"When Scott asked me to put your names on the guest list for the press party, I made a few inquiries," Arno explained. "I make it a point to know something about all my guests. And I would be delighted to introduce you to Mr. McCoy, but as you can see, he's getting in his car now. Perhaps some other time?"

"That's okay," Joe said. "We'll just hang around until he finishes."

Arno flashed a toothy smile. "Say, I've got an idea! We're videotaping his entire lap from my helicopter. Why don't you come along? You can

7

see the whole race course from the air and witness the historic event from the best seats in the house!"

Joe didn't care much for Arno's tone or manner. The slick way he had breezed into town and taken all the credit for Scott's work didn't sit well with Joe. Still, this was too good an opportunity to pass up. "Sounds great," came Joe's reply.

"How about you, Scott? Arno asked, smiling at the young driver.

"No thanks," Scott said, looking Arno straight in the eyes. "I've seen McCoy drive before, and I'm quite familiar with the layout of the course. You and your pals on the city council didn't bother to give me any credit, but those are my course maps you used as the blueprint for the Bayport Grand Prix."

"And I have no great love of flying," Voss said, breaking the awkward silence that followed Scott's quiet outburst. "I like to go fast—but I prefer to do it on the ground."

Joe felt a twinge of guilt as he and Frank moved away from Scott, toward a cargo helicopter that had been modified to hold a video crew and cameras. He almost felt as if he were deserting his friend. Arno hustled them on board and introduced them to a short man with a notepad. "I'd like you to meet T. B. Martin. He's writing McCoy's biography."

The writer wore thick, wire-rim glasses and a photographer's vest crammed with notebooks, pens, and even a small tape recorder. His dark hair and beard were trimmed so short that they bristled. "Actually, I'm just a ghost writer," Martin said. "McCoy will get the credit."

"Oh, so it's supposed to be an autobiography," Frank shouted as the large turbine engine started to wind up.

"Sure, it's an *auto*-biography," Joe cut in, laughing as the lumbering machine lifted off the ground. "McCoy drives *cars* for a living, doesn't he?"

As the helicopter rose higher, Frank could see the whole city of Bayport spread out below, as well as Barmet Bay and the Atlantic Ocean beyond that.

Joe outlined the course for his brother. "It's kind of a sloppy U-shape, with a few squiggles thrown in. It starts at the Bayport Fairgrounds and then runs south through the middle of town and curves around the bay to the ocean.

"Down there," he shouted, pointing again, "it swings back behind the city to the west. Then it runs into the highway and heads up a long straight section due north. Up there, it turns east and runs to the cliffs on the coast north of town. Finally, it swings back along the bay again."

"This course reminds me of Monte Carlo," Martin shouted above the din of the engine and the rotor blades.

Joe focused out the window again and saw

McCoy's race car, a tiny ant-mobile, crawling around the turn at the south end of the course. Now it was heading back inland. Because of the helicopter's height and speed, McCoy seemed to be barely moving, but Joe knew he must be topping 190 as he headed into the long straightaway that ran to the north before the course turned uphill to the northern cliffs at the ocean's edge.

"Yeah," Joe yelled back to Martin. "The only difference is the tunnel at Monte Carlo doesn't lead out into a blind hairpin turn!" He was talking about the tunnel cut through the cliff that ended just before the road made a tight westward turn away from the ocean to follow the curve of Barmet Bay. Everyone in Bayport knew about the hazardous curve. It had been the scene of many accidents over the years—some of them fatal. "If you miss that turn, it's a long, rough ride down to the bottom."

The helicopter swung out over the ocean as McCoy disappeared into the tunnel. It seemed like an eternity before he came out the other end, although it couldn't have been more than a few seconds. The car came rocketing out of the tunnel, hugging the road surface in an impressive display of aerodynamic technology. But something was wrong.

"He's going too fast! He won't make it!" Frank shouted. Before anyone could respond, the car smashed through the guardrail on the hairpin turn.

For a second it looked as if the car could fly. But its forward momentum quickly gave way to the pull of gravity, and the car plummeted toward the cold, waiting waters of the Atlantic two hundred feet below.

The impact with the water barely seemed to slow it down. The car knifed cleanly through the surface—and sank without a trace.

Chapter

2

THE HELICOPTER QUICKLY swooped down to the spot where the race car had plunged into the ocean. Concentric waves rippled across the water, but there was no sign of McCoy or the car. The bullet-shaped vehicle had sliced straight to the bottom.

Frank Hardy looked over to see his brother fumbling at the laces on his shoes. "What are you doing?"

"I'm going in after him!" Joe unbuttoned his shirt as he lunged out of his seat. "He might still be alive, trapped down there!"

Frank leapt up and stepped in front of the sliding cargo door before Joe could reach it. He grabbed his brother by the shoulders. "Stop for a second and think, Joe. The water is at least fifty

feet deep here, and you know what the currents are like.''

Joe struggled against his brother's arms. "We can't just leave him down there!"

Frank pushed Joe away from the door. "The impact from the two-hundred-foot fall probably killed him before the car sank. If you jump in without scuba gear, you'll just beome another casualty.''

"He's right," T. B. Martin agreed grimly. "People like McCoy court death for a living. He knew the risks. Living on the edge was what he was all about. For McCoy, it was fun. But he wouldn't want someone else to risk his own life needlessly.''

Frank put his hand on his brother's shoulder. "Come on, Joe. Sit down. You're not going anywhere.''

Joe's shoulders slumped. He knew they were right—but he couldn't help thinking they had to do *something*.

Frank was one step ahead of him. "Tell the pilot to radio the police and put the chopper down on the road where the car went through the guardrail," Frank said to Arno.

Russell Arno was just staring out at the ocean. He seemed distracted—or maybe it was just the shock of the accident. After a moment Arno nodded and shouted into the pilot's ear.

Frank and Joe were the first ones to jump out of the copter when it touched down. They headed straight for the twisted remains of the guardrail. It looked like a licorice stick that had been casually ripped in half—except this licorice stick was made of steel, Joe reminded himself.

The guardrail wasn't the only thing damaged by the crash. Debris lay all over the place. The thin "wings" attached to the needle-nose front of the race car had been ripped off and were now lying crumpled on either side of the gash in the barrier.

Frank stooped down to examine some of the parts that didn't make the final voyage and were now scattered on the road. There were some shards of glass, a sideview mirror—and something else that caught Frank's eye. He picked it up to inspect it more closely. It appeared to be some kind of electronic device.

"This doesn't look like a normal car part," he mused, thinking out loud.

A voice from behind Frank broke his train of thought. "Nothing on these Formula One machines is 'normal.'" Frank turned to see Arno peering over his shoulder. "This is the cutting edge of automotive high tech," Arno continued. "Half the stuff under the hood is top secret—so the driver can *keep* his edge. McCoy did a lot of his own mechanical work. There's a good chance that the only person who can tell you what you're holding is down there." Arno motioned down to the deceptively calm waters.

Joe looked over at Arno, noting how composed

the promoter seemed, given the circumstances. "You don't seem too concerned about McCoy's death," he said, trying to control his temper.

Arno shrugged. "It's like Martin told you— McCoy lived on the edge. All good racing drivers do. The danger is part of the thrill. Some of these guys, like McCoy, think they're so good they can cheat death. And when you start thinking like that, death sneaks up behind you.

"But you're wrong to think I'm not concerned," Arno added, sadness creeping into his voice for the first time. "McCoy and I worked together a long time. He was a hard man to like, but I'll miss him."

Their conversation was interrupted by the arrival of a squad car carrying two of Bayport's finest. The driver got out and lumbered over to the small group, while the other officer walked toward T. B. Martin to take his statement. The uniformed man who approached Frank and Joe was large, more than a little out of shape, and sported a sizable paunch. Joe wondered how he managed to keep his pants up, before he noticed his nameplate: "Reed."

"Okay," Officer Reed huffed. "What happened here?"

Before either Frank or Joe could say anything, Arno started in. "A tragic accident," he began smoothly. "Mr. McCoy miscalculated the turn, and at one hundred fifty miles per hour it was a deadly mistake."

"Stupid race car drivers," Reed grumbled. "There's a reason for the posted speed limit, you know."

"At the posted speed limit"—Arno jerked his thumb back toward the sign that said 15 MPH—"the engine would have stalled out, and he would have had to push the car around the turn. That would *not* have produced a spectacular lap time."

The police officer looked back toward the tunnel, and then his eyes moved from the tunnel exit to the gaping hole in the guardrail. "Well, what kind of lap time do you suppose he'll get now?" He frowned. "The only thing 'spectacular' here was his crash. Maybe they'll cancel that stupid race now."

"I doubt it," Arno said curtly as he walked away.

"What do you think of this?" Frank said, holding out the electronic device he had found.

"What am I supposed to think?" the police officer retorted gruffly. "Some stupid gizmo to make a car go too fast and ruin a perfectly good guardrail. This is going to cost the county plenty, you know."

Frank and Joe gave the officer their statements, and then Reed lumbered off to join his partner, who was radioing in a report to headquarters. Frank surveyed the scene again, then turned to his brother. "I don't like this."

"Who does?" Joe responded grimly.

"Come on," Frank said, tugging at his brother's arm, "I want to ask Martin a few questions. Something just doesn't add up."

The Hardys approached the writer, who was standing by the edge of the cliff. He was staring into the blue waters below. "Excuse me, Mr. Martin," Frank said quietly, "but I was wondering if I could ask you something."

"You know," the writer began in a distracted tone, "you think you're prepared for this sort of thing. After ten years of covering the racing circuit, you think you've seen it all. Guys get killed every year. No big surprise. But somehow, you're never really ready when it happens."

He was silent for a moment, then he said, "I'm sorry. What was it you wanted to know?"

"Were the two of you close?" Frank asked.

"Close?" Martin repeated. "Nobody was close to Angus McCoy. Everything was a competition for him. He never let up, never wanted to lose the edge.

"You know, he hated having a ghost writer, wanted to do the book himself. But his publisher saw the first couple of chapters and had the ugly task of telling Angus he couldn't write worth beans. If it weren't for the contract, he would have fired the publisher."

"What happens to the book now?" Frank pressed. "Will the publisher cancel it?"

"Are you kidding?" Martin laughed. "This is the kind of ending publishers dream about! I can just see the title now: *The Fast Life and Tragic*

Death of Angus McCoy! And we've got the whole thing on videotape! The publisher will love it. Pictures of the famous racing driver's last moments! It'll sell millions!''

The writer laughed again, but both Frank and Joe could see the laughter was forced and bitter. Martin turned back toward the ocean and was silent for a while. Finally he said, ''Does that answer your question?''

''Actually, that wasn't the question I wanted to ask,'' Frank said apologetically. ''Something just doesn't make any sense to me. McCoy knew the layout of the course, right?''

''Sure. He'd driven it several times to get familiar with it,'' Martin said.

''And he didn't really have any serious competition in this race, right?''

''Right.''

''So why would he push so hard? And why did he drive as though he didn't know the turn was there?''

''The answer to the first question is easy.'' Martin smiled. ''Race drivers always push hard. They're not just racing against other drivers and the clock—they're competing against themselves.

''Angus was getting a little old for the game,'' Martin went on. ''There were guys who said he was all washed up, so he had something to prove. As for your second question,'' the writer continued after a brief pause, ''I don't have an answer. Angus was a much better driver than on that last turn. And it's not like this is the only course with a hairpin turn."

He shrugged. "Angus was a world champion. I don't understand it, either. This is the kind of mistake a newcomer would make."

"What about sabotage?" Frank ventured.

The question surprised both Martin and Joe. "Who would have a motive?" Joe cut in.

"Somebody who wants to win," Frank replied simply.

At that moment Russell Arno joined them at the cliff's edge. He kicked at a small rock, and Joe watched it roll and bounce down the steep incline. He barely made out the tiny splash it made when it hit the water below.

Arno turned to him and casually said, "Well, now that McCoy is out of it, it looks like your friend Scott Lavin is the new favorite."

Chapter
3

THE NEXT DAY was one of those late-summer days when the sun felt somehow cooler, even though the temperature was as hot as mid-July.

Joe Hardy was sitting on his front porch, thinking that even the shadows cast by the sun were different at this time of year. Softer. Maybe the morning seemed special because he knew summer was almost over. But Joe was sure he could recognize this kind of day even if he were set down in the middle of it, without anyone telling him what season it was.

Joe had been up for a while. The day before had been long, but he had slept well. Joe rarely had trouble sleeping. There wasn't any problem that wasn't easier to tackle after a good night's sleep, he thought.

Frank Hardy emerged from the house about

one o'clock, stretching and yawning. "You look like you could use a couple more hours of sack time," Joe remarked.

"I was up most of the night doing some work on the computer," Frank explained. The Hardys had a sophisticated computer setup, complete with a telephone modem to access other computers, and they often used it to help solve cases. If information was available over a phone link-up, Frank knew how to get at it.

"It took quite a while," Frank went on, "but I found out some interesting things. About Scott Lavin," he added.

"Oh?" Joe said, raising his eyebrows. "Let's hear it."

"Building and racing Formula One cars is very expensive," Frank began. "It takes a lot of money—and that means sponsors and investors. Scott got started with seed money from a few investors, but that money is almost gone now. He's been looking for sponsors—advertisers who will pay him to promote their products. But Scott doesn't have enough of a reputation on the Grand Prix circuit yet. He needs a big win to get that rep."

"Go on." Joe fought to keep his voice cool. Scott Lavin was his friend, and he didn't like where this conversation was leading.

"Look, Joe, I know how you feel about Scott," Frank said softly. "But right now he's the only suspect we've got. I think we should investigate."

"Suspect? Investigate?" Joe forgot about being cool. "What are you talking about? How do you know McCoy's death wasn't an accident? And even if it wasn't, Scott wouldn't murder anyone just to win a race. Besides, he's a top-notch driver and had a shot at winning—even with McCoy in the race."

Frank looked at his younger brother. He knew Joe was smart, but sometimes Joe's short fuse didn't allow him the logic to think things through. "You don't believe that crash was an accident any more than I do," Frank told him. "He hit that guardrail like it had a bull's-eye painted on it. Either he was struck by a sudden suicidal urge or there was something wrong with his car."

"Like what?" Joe demanded.

"I don't know. The brakes or the steering, probably. Take a look at this thing." Frank was holding the electronic device he had found at the crash site. "What does it look like to you? It looks like part of a radio-control setup to me. Flip a switch and *zap!* No more brakes."

Frank could see doubt flicker in his brother's eyes. "There's something you're forgetting," he continued. "Scott is probably bitter about this whole race. This is his course and his hometown, and Arno and McCoy just walked in and took away the spotlight. That's got to hurt.

"Maybe the money and the sponsorship wouldn't be enough, but throw in a little need for revenge. Maybe that pushed Scott over the edge.''

There was an awkward silence after Frank finished talking. "You're all wrong about Scott," Joe snapped. "You could be right about the crash. It didn't look like an accident exactly, but I think we should check out some other people first.''

"Okay," Frank said. "Who?"

"Well, what about this Arno character?''

"The promoter? What's his motive?''

"He said he had a 'financial interest' in Mc-Coy.''

"Yeah. An interest in keeping him alive to bring in the big attendance on race day. What does he gain by McCoy's death?''

"I don't know," Joe admitted with a sigh. "I guess it wouldn't hurt to start by talking to Scott.''

After eating a late lunch, the Hardys drove over to Scott Lavin's garage and parked their van outside. They walked in the open door and found Scott and his head mechanic hunched over the engine of the yellow-and-red race car. Joe took one look at the machine, and some of the excitement of the previous day returned. Ever since he could remember, he had been in love with cars, and he couldn't help but share his enthusiasm with his brother.

"The wings at the front end and behind the

23

rear tires act just like the wings on an airplane, only in reverse," Joe said. "They create negative lift, thousands of pounds of downforce to keep the car on the road in high-speed turns.

"And see those side panels sticking out from the chassis, running the length of the car? They look like jet engines or something, but they're really upside-down airfoils. They scoop up air through intakes in the front and create an area of low pressure underneath, sucking the car to the road surface like a vacuum cleaner. It's called ground effects."

"If you're going fast enough," Scott Lavin said, not even looking up from his work, "you can generate enough downforce to ride a track upside-down. At least, that's what the designers tell me. I've never actually tried it."

Scott stood up, wiped his hands on a rag, and smiled at the Hardys. "Formula One racing entered the space age back in the late sixties when airplane designers started tinkering with Grand Prix cars. The old stainless steel carrot is still under there, somewhere, buried in state-of-the-art aerodynamics. Except it's not even stainless steel anymore. It's aluminum and high-tech fibers with names you can't pronounce.

"Just about the only old-fashioned part is the open cockpit. It seems as if it would make more sense to cover it with a smooth canopy—just as they've covered everything else."

"Except the tires, of course. The tires are

something of a technological feat themselves," Joe said.

Frank noticed that the rear tires were larger than the front ones and almost twice as wide. "Almost no tread," he observed.

"Touch one of them," Scott suggested. "It's a special rubber. It's sticky. At the end of a race the rubber looks like it's about ready to drip off the wheels. The tires last only about three hundred miles. One race and that's it."

Joe pointed to the V-8 engine. "This is a little old-fashioned, too. They've eliminated turbo-charged engines."

Scott nodded. "They were generating just too much power. Formula One racing was getting too dangerous."

"As if it isn't dangerous now," Frank said, thinking of Angus McCoy's car at the bottom of the Atlantic Ocean. "It looks a lot like the cars they drive at the Indianapolis 500."

"It *is* a lot like an Indy car," Scott agreed. "There's a lot of cross-breeding between Grand Prix and Indianapolis. Rear-mounted engines, wings, and ground effects were all developed in Formula One before making the jump to Indy. Indy cars outweigh Formula One cars by about three hundred pounds—even though they carry less fuel and have smaller wings."

"Why the differences?" Frank asked.

"Different conditions," Joe said. "There are no pit stops in a two-hundred-fifty-mile Grand

Prix race, so you have to start with all the fuel you're going to need. And the wings on a Formula One car have to handle a lot of different and tight turns. Indy cars go in one direction around nice, banked oval curves."

"All of this technology must take a lot of money," Frank commented, looking at Scott.

Scott laughed and said, "There's an old saying in racing circles: 'Speed costs money. How fast do you want to go?' " He glanced from one brother to the other. "Did you guys come down here to discuss my finances?"

"No, no," Joe replied quickly. "We just came by to see how things were going."

"Well, they could be better," Scott said.

"Was everybody pretty shook up about the crash yesterday?" Frank ventured.

"I hate to sound callous," Scott responded, "but that's the least of my problems. I feel bad about McCoy, but the show goes on. This is a dangerous profession. At Indy, if there's a big accident on the course, they delay the race until they clear away the wreckage. In a Grand Prix race, they just stick in a guy with a flag to warn you that you're about to drive into a disaster area. McCoy's not the first world champion to die in his car—not even the first to die during time trials.

"I guess if they got really concerned about the dangers, they'd stop having races on the open road. But Grand Prix racing is just starting to catch on in the U.S. now. Cities like Dallas and Detroit realized they could make money off Formula One racing without spending any money to build a track.

"These cars may be safer than they were twenty years ago, but fatal crashes still aren't all that unusual. A lot of drivers *assume* that's how they'll go."

Scott scowled. "My problem is far more immediate and practical. One of my crew just up and quit, and we still have a lot of work to do." He paused for a second, then looked at Joe. "Hey, Joe, you said you wanted to get your hands on one of these babies. Here's your chance. It's not driving, but it's hands-on experience. How would you like to join my crew for a few days? Just until the race is over."

"Sure!" Joe blurted out, before his brother had a chance to say anything.

Frank glanced at Joe out of the corner of his eye and then shifted his attention back to Scott. "Actually, we *did* want to ask you a few questions, Scott," he began.

"No problem," Scott interrupted. "Maybe later. Right now Joe and I have a lot of work to do. Right, Joe?"

Joe hesitated for a moment, torn between his brother and something he had dreamed about—the chance to be part of a Grand Prix racing team. Maybe McCoy's crash *had* been a simple accident, he told himself. Even if it wasn't, Scott couldn't be responsible for it. Suddenly, finding out who *was* responsible didn't seem so important.

"Right!" Joe heard himself say, agreeing with Scott.

Scott Lavin put his arm around Joe's shoulder, and together they walked away from Frank.

Chapter

4

AFTER CHECKING OUT the garage for an hour or so, Frank left alone. He didn't know if he should be mad at Joe or worried or both. There's no hard evidence against Scott Lavin, he reminded himself. But Joe's judgment was clouded by friendship and fast cars. If Scott's setting him up for some reason, Joe won't see it coming. In fact, Scott could have offered Joe a job just to get us off the case. Scott knows our reputation.

All these concerns ran through Frank's head as he got in the van and drove off in the direction of Phil Cohen's house. At a traffic light he opened the glove compartment and checked to make sure the electronic device was still where he'd put it before going into Scott Lavin's garage.

Frank didn't know a lot about race cars, but he was sure this thing didn't belong on one. It looked jury-rigged from something intended for another purpose. But what was its purpose now? Frank still didn't know.

If anyone could find out, it was their old friend, Phil Cohen. Anything Phil didn't know about electronics wasn't worth knowing. Frank parked the van in front of the Cohens' house, took the metal object out of the glove compartment, and walked toward the front door. A passing car caught his eye—a silver gray Lotus sport coupe. Not too many cars like that around Bayport, Frank thought.

He shrugged off a nagging feeling that he had seen the car before and rang the doorbell. No one answered. He waited a minute and then tried knocking. Still no response. Frank started to walk back toward the van, and then he realized that Phil was probably out in the garage.

Phil's passion for electronic gizmos had threatened to engulf the Cohen house. They spilled out of Phil's bedroom and into the guest room. Finally, his folks had exiled his electrical empire to the garage, which was fine with Phil. It meant he could work late at night without waking anybody up.

Frank followed the path from the house to the door on the side of the garage. He could hear Phil singing inside. "Sounds more like a goose honking," Frank muttered. "But at least it means Phil's home."

Frank knocked on the side door. No answer,

Phil just kept singing. Frank knocked again and was greeted by more loud goose noises. He tried the handle. The door was unlocked. He pushed it open and saw Phil sitting at a workbench, facing away from the door, wearing a pair of small headphones from a portable cassette player.

Something's strange about those headphones, Frank thought. But what? He looked more closely. There were no wires leading to the cassette player lying on the workbench. But Phil was obviously listening to something because his head was nodding in time to a beat Frank couldn't hear.

Frank walked over and tapped Phil on the shoulder. Phil jumped up, knocking his chair over in the process. "What—" he exclaimed. "Oh, it's you," he shouted over the music in his ears.

Phil took off the headphones and handed them to Frank. "Check this out. I'm working on a set of cordless headphones. Not exactly a radical concept, except I'm trying to come up with an infrared sender-receiver small enough for a hand-held portable cassette player."

Frank noticed that the tape player on the bench was wired up to a black box with an infrared sensor. The box was larger than the tape player. "Still needs some work," Frank observed.

"Yeah. Well, but you know me—I'll just keep hacking away until I figure it out. Then I'll patent it and retire on the royalties." Phil grinned.

"Think you could figure *this* out?" Frank

asked, handing over the piece of evidence from the fatal crash.

Phil took it, turned it over, inspected the connections of a few of the exposed wires, set it down on the workbench, and began methodically attacking it with a screwdriver. He took off the face plate and revealed several intricate circuit boards. After fiddling with it for a few minutes he said, "I'm not sure. It could be some kind of radio receiver."

Frank nodded. "That's what I thought. But to receive what kind of signal?"

Phil shrugged. "I'd have to run some tests, check out a few things. What's this all about, Frank?"

Frank told Phil everything he knew, and then something clicked in his head. "Check it out completely, Phil. Let me know what you find out."

"It could take a while."

"That's okay. I'll call you later. Right now there's something I have to do."

Frank got back in the van and started driving toward the Bayport Fairgrounds, which had been temporarily transformed into makeshift garages and pits for the race. Something Phil had said about royalties reminded him of the writer, T. B. Martin. Frank was hoping he could find him at the fairgrounds.

It wasn't a straight drive to the fairgrounds. Like much of downtown Bayport, the fairgrounds were blocked off from regular traffic for the duration of the race. Frank parked the van about half a mile away and walked the rest of the distance. He didn't get there until seven o'clock.

He found Martin in the aluminum shed that served as the portable garage for McCoy Racing. The writer was talking to Reinhart Voss, the number-two man on the McCoy team. Martin recognized Frank and waved him over. "Frank Hardy, right? I wanted to talk to you and your brother. I'm working on the final chapter of McCoy's biography. It may sound gruesome, but I want to get eyewitness descriptions from everybody who saw the crash."

"Let's make a trade," Frank replied. "Answer a few questions for me, and I'll tell you what I saw."

"Sounds good. What can I tell you now that you didn't get out of me yesterday? You guys sure ask a lot of questions. Maybe *you* should be writing a book."

"Will you make royalties off the sales of McCoy's biography?" Frank asked.

"Posthumous autobiography," Martin corrected him. "Sure. For every copy sold, I'll make a few cents. It won't make me rich, but if the book hits the best-seller charts, I won't have to worry about a paycheck for a while."

"What happens to McCoy's share of the profits now that he's dead? Do you get it all?"

The writer eyed Frank suspiciously. "If you're

asking if I'd benefit from McCoy's death, the answer is no. Dead or alive, McCoy's share goes to a company called Clarco Industries. It's in the contract.''

Martin paused and then said, "What are you getting at, anyway? The crash was an accident, wasn't it? Do you know something that I don't?''

"Nothing yet," Frank responded. He noticed that it was starting to get dark out. "Listen, it's getting late. I've got to go.''

"Okay—but you owe me an interview!" Martin called after him as Frank headed out the door.

Somehow the day had gotten away from Frank. The late start threw him off. He jogged back to the van. It was dusk, and he had to turn on the headlights for the drive back to Scott Lavin's garage. He knew that Scott and his crew would be finishing sometime soon, and he wanted to be there when Scott closed up the garage.

Unlike the out-of-town drivers and racing teams that had to make do with temporary arrangements on the fairgrounds, Scott still kept a private garage in Bayport. Frank had noticed a sophisticated burglar alarm system on his earlier visit, and that was what interested him now.

Frank pulled the van into a dark alley across from the garage, took out a pair of binoculars, and waited. Finally three figures emerged. One of them was the mechanic, one was Scott Lavin, and the third was Joe Hardy. Frank felt bad. He was spying on his own brother.

Frank lifted the binoculars and focused on Scott. The burglar alarm control panel was on the outside of the garage. Anyone trying to get in couldn't even open the doors for a second without setting off the alarm. Scott opened the control box, and Frank shifted the binoculars slightly to zoom in on the control panel. There was a calculator-style keypad with an LED display screen at the top. Even in the dark, Frank could see the sequence of glowing numbers that Scott quickly punched in: 3-3-1-4-6-1. The alarm was activated, and Scott closed the control box.

Frank watched the trio depart and then waited a few more minutes. He climbed between the two front seats into the back of the van and opened the tool chest. "Let's see, I'll need the flashlight—and this—" he muttered, taking out a flat case and slipping it into his back pocket. Then he opened the back door of the van, hopped lightly to the ground, and closed the door softly.

He walked across the street casually, approaching Scott's garage as if he owned the place. Frank strolled right up to the burglar alarm and flipped open the control box. He looked around to make sure no one was in sight. Then he turned back to the control panel and punched in the same sequence of numbers Scott had used earlier: 3-3-1-4-6-1. Finally he pressed the Alarm Off button. The burglar alarm was now deactivated. No problem.

Now came the tricky part. The door was

locked, of course, but Frank was prepared. He reached into his back pocket and pulled out the soft leather case that he had taken from the tool chest. Unsnapping the cover, he opened the case, revealing an assortment of thin metal strips in a variety of lengths and widths—a lock-pick set.

Breaking and entering didn't rate high on Frank's list of favorite investigative techniques. If things had gone down differently, he might have had Joe set up a diversion while he searched the place in broad daylight. But he was working alone now, and he didn't have a whole lot of time. In a few days the race would be over, and Scott Lavin would pack up and head out for the next Grand Prix race, probably in another country. Any chance of uncovering evidence would be gone.

Frank wasn't planning on taking anything. He was just going to look around—to see if he could find any radio equipment that might provide a link to the mysterious device now in Phil Cohen's workshop.

He worked the lock like an expert. The Bayport police frequently gave home security seminars, complete with demonstrations of the various burglary tools used to break into houses. Frank always made it a point to attend the classes.

The lock mechanism began to turn, and he felt the deadbolt slide back. He slowly turned the doorknob and then eased the door open. He slipped into the garage and closed the door quickly, feeling certain he had avoided detection.

The garage was pitch-black, but Frank wasn't going to turn on the lights. He didn't want to attract attention. He switched on the flashlight, and abruptly the garage came alive with shadows that wavered and jumped as Frank moved the beam around in the dark, scanning all the unfamiliar machinery. He spotted what appeared to be a pile of electrical equipment and figured that it was as good a place as any to start looking.

Then Frank heard it—a faint noise behind him, like a shoe being scuffed on the cement floor. He stiffened, realizing suddenly that he'd forgotten to lock the door behind him.

Pivoting on one foot, he whirled to face whoever it was and caught a blow to the side of his head. He tottered on his feet for a second—then Frank Hardy's world faded to black.

Chapter

5

IT WAS LATE when Joe Hardy got home. He walked in the front door and headed for the kitchen in search of something to eat. He found his aunt Gertrude making a cup of tea. "Sorry I missed dinner," Joe said as he opened the refrigerator. "Anything left to eat?"

"Well, at least you called," Gertrude said. "Here it is, already past nine, and your brother isn't home yet. He missed dinner and didn't even call. You two went out together this afternoon. What happened?"

"Nothing much." Joe grabbed a loaf of bread and some peanut butter. "We went to see Scott Lavin, and then I hung around to help out with Scott's car. Frank took off in the van. He didn't tell me where he was going. I figured he was headed back here."

"Did you two have a fight?" Gertrude asked, a hint of concern edging into her voice.

Joe took a big bite of his sandwich to buy time while he chose his words. Finally he said, "I wouldn't call it a *fight,* exactly. We just didn't agree."

"Oh?" Gertrude replied. "And what, exactly, didn't you agree about?"

Just then the telephone rang. Joe jumped up and said, "I'll get it!" And then he muttered under his breath, "Saved by the bell."

"Hardy summer home," Joe spoke into the receiver. "Some are home and some aren't."

"Hi, Joe. Is Frank there?"

Joe recognized the voice right away. "Hey, Phil. No, he's not here. And I don't know where he is. Did you see him at all today?"

"Yeah," Phil said. "He came by this afternoon. There was something he wanted me to check out. Have him call me when he gets in, okay?"

"Sure thing," Joe said. "Say, did Frank tell you where he was going when he left your house? Aunt Gertrude's getting a little worried about him," he added in a soft voice so Gertrude wouldn't overhear.

"No—he just said there was something else he had to do. I doubt if that's much help."

"Maybe more than you think," Joe said. "Thanks, Phil."

He hung up the phone and turned to his aunt. "I've got to go out again."

"What for?" Gertrude asked suspiciously.

"I think I left something at Scott's place," came the reply as Joe shot out the front door.

"Couldn't it wait until tomorrow?" Gertrude called after him. But there was no answer. Joe was gone.

Joe didn't know where Frank had gone after he'd left Phil, but he had a hunch where his brother might be now. Since Frank had taken the van, Joe had to walk. He could have asked his parents for their car, but he didn't want them asking any questions. Aunt Gertrude's were bad enough.

Besides, he wasn't sure if his hunch was right. And if it was, what was he supposed to tell his aunt? He shook his head as he imagined himself saying, "Gee, Aunt Gertrude, I think Frank's trying to break into Scott's garage, and I just thought I'd go down to see if he needs any help."

Somehow he doubted that that would make his aunt feel any better. Of course, the only "help" he intended to give Frank was to try to stop him before it was too late.

Joe wasn't sure what Frank was up to, but he knew his older brother pretty well. If Joe was right, he wanted to get there before anybody else did. He broke into a jog as he backtracked along the route he had taken just a little while earlier.

Joe was breathing heavily by the time he

reached Scott Lavin's garage. He slowed to a walk about twenty yards from the door and let himself catch his breath as he scanned the area. His eyes had adjusted to the dark, and he could make out the faint outline of the van in the alley across the street. He headed for the van and tried the door.

Locked. Joe pulled his key chain out of his pocket, fumbling in the dark for the right key. He opened the van door and poked his head inside. Frank wasn't there, but Joe did notice something in the back of the van.

The tool chest was open. Joe climbed inside and over the front seat, switching on the overhead light as he went. He already suspected what he would find in the tool chest—or, more exactly, what he *wouldn't* find. He was right—the lock-pick set was missing.

Joe climbed out of the van and doubled back across the street in the direction of Scott Lavin's garage. From the middle of the street he could now see that the door to the garage was ajar, even though all the lights were out.

A mental warning alarm went off in Joe's brain. Frank wouldn't be so careless. The slightly open door was as obvious as a flashing neon sign proclaiming, "Burglars at work!" Joe stood at the threshold and tried to get a look inside the garage, but his eyes couldn't penetrate the darkness within. He drew in a deep breath, gritted his teeth, plunged through the door—and almost tripped over his brother's body, slumped on the floor.

Frank Hardy struggled through a fog to see his brother's face staring down at him. "Joe?" he croaked. "What happened?"

Joe was sitting cross-legged on the floor, cradling Frank's head in his lap. "You almost got yourself killed from the looks of it," he said.

"Somebody knocked me out!" Frank exclaimed, struggling to sit up as the mist started to clear from his brain.

"Yeah," Joe agreed. "*You* did." He pointed to a heavy duty hoist and a racing engine lying on its side on the garage floor, under a single light that he had switched on. "You must have tripped the hoist release by accident, stumbling around in the dark like a blind cat burglar. If you'd been standing a little more to the left, that engine would have done more than just knock you out before it crashed into the floor."

"How did you know where to find me?" Frank asked as Joe helped him get up.

"It wasn't too hard," Joe snapped. "Phil couldn't tell you if there was any connection between that hunk of electronics you found and McCoy's accident, so you came back here, hoping to dig up some other evidence. But you're on the wrong track this time."

Frank rubbed his aching head—and remembered something. "There was somebody else in the garage. I heard him—just before my lights went out. He whacked me on the side of the head, and then he must have released the engine from the hoist to make it look like an accident.''

"Just look at that engine," Joe said. "We'll be lucky to get it fixed before the race. You can't blame this on Scott."

He scowled and stared around the garage. "You know, Frank, there are other drivers besides Scott in this race. Maybe somebody *did* sabotage McCoy's car, but it wasn't Scott."

"Maybe I was getting too close to the truth," Frank persisted, "and Scott trashed his own engine to put me out of commission and throw me off the trail at the same time."

Joe's anger blew away his concern for his brother. "You don't give up, do you?" he shouted. "I *know* Scott Lavin, and I'm telling you he didn't do it!"

"And I might have known I'd find the two of you here," another voice interrupted. Frank and Joe whirled around to see police officer Con Riley. "If there's trouble in Bayport, the Hardy brothers can't be far away."

Riley hoisted the service revolver that he had pointed at the Hardys a moment before. "But somehow I can't see the pair of you as car thieves," he continued. "Someone reported seeing a prowler break in here, and I arrive on the scene to find Frank and Joe Hardy. I can't wait to hear the explanation."

If the Hardys had a friend on the Bayport police force, it was Con Riley. Riley would be willing to cut them a little slack, but he wouldn't let them walk away from a breaking and entering charge—at least, not without a *really* good explanation.

Before Frank could say anything, Joe started talking. "I'm working for Scott Lavin, helping him get ready for the race," he said quickly. "I came back to finish up some work."

Riley glanced at the damaged engine lying on the floor. "Scott's really going to appreciate your dedication," he observed dryly. He looked around some more and said, "I don't see any signs of forced entry, but why don't we give Scott a call and check out your story?"

"Sure." Frank abruptly changed the subject. "Say, Con, do you know if the divers have recovered Angus McCoy's body yet?"

"Not yet, and they probably never will."

"Why? What do you mean?"

"They finally did find the car, but the body wasn't there. They think the currents must have carried it out to sea."

"I don't get it." Joe frowned. "He was strapped in with a double shoulder harness, a lap belt, and leg straps. How could the body go anywhere?"

Riley shrugged. "He was a race car driver and trained to react quickly in emergencies. Maybe he popped the belt releases, hoping he could survive the crash if he didn't go down with the car. Now I think you boys had better make that call to Lavin."

But before they could find a phone, Riley was interrupted by the squawk of his two-way radio. "All units in the vicinity of the twenty-four-hundred block of Grant Street," the radio blared, "proceed to two-four-oh-two. We have a report of a three-alarm fire. Repeat: fire at two-four-oh-two Grant Street."

"That address sounds familiar," Joe said.

"Twenty-four-oh-two Grant? That's Phil Cohen's house!" Frank shouted. "Phil's house is on fire!"

Chapter

6

"COME ON, LET'S GO!" Frank Hardy shouted, sprinting for the van. "We've got to get to Phil's right away!"

Joe and Con were just a split second slower in reacting to the radio report of the fire at Phil's house. Joe followed Riley to his squad car and grabbed the officer's arm before he slipped into the driver's seat. "Look, I know this isn't exactly normal police procedure—but do me a favor."

"Now what?" Riley asked impatiently.

Just then Frank backed the van out of the alley and yelled, "Joe, you coming or not?"

Joe nodded quickly, then turned back to Riley and said, "Phil's our friend, and Frank has his reasons for wanting to get there in a hurry. So how about giving us a police escort on the streets that are blocked off for the race?"

"What?" Riley responded in disbelief.

"Could you lead the way?"

Riley stared at him for a moment. "Okay. But just this once!"

Joe smiled and said, "Anything you say, *Officer* Riley." He dashed over to the van, but instead of going around to the passenger's side, he opened the driver's door and said, "Move over, brother, I'm driving."

Frank didn't have time to protest. Joe backed up his instruction with a firm shove, then scrambled into the driver's seat. The cruiser was pulling away from the curb, lights flashing and siren blaring. Joe slammed the van into gear and took off after it.

"What's the big idea?" Frank complained. "Don't like my driving?"

"No, no," Joe said. "I think you're a great defensive driver, but this calls for a little more *aggressive* driving. Like racing."

"And you've had so much racing experience since you got your regular license this year," Frank replied sarcastically. "In fact, now that I think about it, I've been driving twice as long as you have!"

"Yeah—but Scott told me about a few racing tricks today," Joe said as he edged the car over into the left lane, braking slightly at the same time. Then he shifted his right foot back to the gas pedal and started to speed up as he followed the police car into a right-hand turn. The maneuver cut the distance between the two vehicles in half.

"Do your braking *before* the turn," Joe explained as the van continued to pursue Riley's cruiser. "Enter the turn from the far side to reduce the angle and gradually accelerate through the curve—so that you're pretty much at full throttle when you come out of the turn."

"A nice trick—as long as nobody's coming at you in the left lane."

"Okay," Joe admitted. "So it's only practical when all the cars are going the same way—or when the street's blocked off to all traffic."

Joe swung the van all the way over to the far right side of the road. Ahead of them, Riley's police car skidded through a left turn, and the van followed close behind. But instead of skidding, Joe took a low angle into the curve, drifting slightly across the yellow median before nosing back into the right lane.

As they came out of the turn, the van was just about touching the rear bumper of the squad car. "What do you think you're doing now?" Frank burst out, his right foot instinctively reaching for a brake pedal that wasn't there.

"This is Grant Street," Joe said. "Home stretch!" Then he punched the gas pedal to the floor and swerved into the left lane just as Frank thought they would rear-end Riley's car. Even though the police car was still accelerating, the van was going even faster, and it shot out in front as Joe brought it back into the right lane.

"I didn't know this van had that much power," Frank said in wonder.

"It doesn't," Joe replied as the van slowed to enter Grant Street. "It's *air* power. The car in front acts as an air-breaker—cutting down wind resistance and leaving a vacuum for the car behind it. You can accelerate faster and build up enough momentum to push ahead. They call it slipstreaming. Neat, huh?" He brought the van to a halt behind a lime green fire engine.

Frank didn't respond. His attention was riveted on a small fire blazing away next to Phil's house. The house wasn't on fire—only one half of the garage. He jumped out of the van and ran over to the nearest fire fighter. "Was anyone hurt?" he asked.

"Doesn't look like it," the man said. "The neighbors said the folks that live here are on vacation, and it's only the garage, anyway."

Frank clutched the man's arm, almost pulling him off balance and shouting, "You mean nobody went inside to check?"

Joe was right behind Frank then. "What's the story?" Joe asked.

Frank whirled around to face his brother. "Phil's folks are out of town—but Phil didn't go with them. He might still be in his workshop, and that's in the garage!"

The two brothers glanced at each other. Without saying anything they both bolted toward the side door of the garage. Con Riley, who had joined them, realized what they were doing and grabbed a hose from a surprised fire fighter. He aimed the nozzle at the boys, soaking Joe and Frank with water before they crashed into the garage.

Through the smoke they could just make out Phil's limp form on the floor. They crawled to him so they remained down low where there was less smoke. But still the heavy black air seared their throats, making them cough uncontrollably. They were half-blind, their eyes stinging and clouding over with tears. Frank grabbed Phil's left arm and Joe took his right, and together they started to drag their unconscious friend toward the side door. The front doors were already a wall of flames.

But it was too late. A burning rafter crashed down just in front of them, sealing the exit. The intense heat and smoke made it hard to breathe and impossible to talk. Frank looked around desperately, knowing that if either he or Joe passed out now, all three of them would die.

They were surrounded by flames now. But Frank spotted a window where the fire was less intense. He ripped one of the wet sleeves off his shirt and wrapped it around the lower part of his face, covering his nose and mouth. He motioned to Joe to do the same, then pointed to the window.

Joe looked at the window. It was about three feet wide and four feet off the ground. He gave his brother the okay sign, got into a linebacker's crouch, held his breath, and ran straight for the window. He took a flying leap, shielded his head with his arms, and crashed through the glass. Just before he hit the ground outside he did a tuck and roll, landing on his feet on the grass.

The fire fighters were stunned by Joe's sudden appearance, but what he did next was even more stunning. He ran back to the burning garage, ripping the cloth off his face and tearing it in half. Joe wrapped the two pieces of cloth around his hands and smashed out the glass shards that jutted up and out from the shattered opening.

Frank couldn't see what was going on outside, but he knew that his brother had made it through the window. At lease *one* of us will come out of this alive, he grimly told himself, grabbing Phil under the arms and dragging him toward the window. Coughing and gasping for breath, Frank kicked and shoved burning debris out of the way as he made a narrow path through the flames.

It seemed as if it took forever to reach the window. By the time he finally made it there, Frank was too tired to push his unconscious friend through to safety. He hoped someone on the other side would help with the job.

Joe reached in to grab Phil's body. Frank smiled weakly and let his brother take the burden off his hands. Even though he felt as if he was about to pass out, Frank couldn't leave the inferno yet.

After Joe hauled Phil through the window, he carried him over to the waiting paramedics. Then he sprinted back to help his brother. But Frank wasn't there. Desperately, Joe tried to scramble back inside the burning garage. Con Riley ran over, grabbed Joe's arm, and yanked him away.

"Back off!" Joe yelled. "Frank's still in there!"

"There's nothing you can do now!" Riley insisted. "The fire's out of control!"

Joe stared numbly. "He was right here at the window. Then he was gone." Fatigue and smoke inhalation were starting to take their toll, but Joe fought back. "I can't leave him in there! Help me or get out of my way!" He pushed Riley aside so hard that Con fell down.

Joe gripped the broken frame with both hands. He put his right foot on the sill and was about to pull himself up and in when he heard a raspy voice croak, "Got an air conditioner on you, brother? It's *hot* in here."

With a final surge of energy, Joe Hardy hauled his brother Frank out just before the roof caved in.

They both lay on the grass, exhausted, ignoring the fire fighters scurrying back and forth in a vain attempt to put out the fire. After a few minutes, Frank sat up, wiped some of the soot off his face, and said, "What happened to Phil? Is he okay?"

At that, Joe jumped up and kicked his brother in the shin. "Ow!" Frank yelled. "What was that for?"

"You don't care about Phil," Joe shouted.

"What do you mean?"

"I mean you were more concerned about that electronic gizmo than you were about Phil."

"Now, wait a min—"

"No, *you* wait," Joe shouted. "You went back to get that thing, didn't you? Phil could have been dying for all you knew, and I could have gotten myself killed."

Frank looked closely at his brother. They were both tired and upset, but Frank struggled to remain levelheaded. "That 'thing,' as you put it, is the *only* thing that could have led us to the person who just tried to kill our friend."

He should have let it go at that, but Joe's accusation had pushed the wrong button, and Frank pushed back. The words seemed to take on a life of their own, and he heard himself saying, "Of course, you seem to be more concerned about helping the guy who might have done it."

Frank was sorry as soon as the words left his mouth, but he couldn't bring himself to apologize. He saw Joe clench his right hand into a fist, and he tried to remember the last time he had gotten into a fistfight with his brother.

Frank didn't want that. He knew he could easily deflect the blow, but he just stood there and waited for it to happen. Maybe he deserved a good punch. Maybe they would both feel better afterward. He didn't know anymore—he just wanted to lie down and go to sleep.

It took Joe a few seconds to realize what he was about to do. He stared down in disbelief at his own balled fist. Was he actually going to hit his brother? No. He commanded the tensed muscles in his arm to relax. Just let it go, he told himself. Just walk away.

Before Frank could say he was sorry, Joe had turned his back and disappeared into the night.

Chapter

7

JOE HARDY STOMPED OFF, angry and confused. His gut instinct told him that Scott Lavin was innocent, but he couldn't just dismiss his brother's suspicions.

First the fatal crash of McCoy's race car, then the "accident" at Scott's garage, and finally the fire at Phil Cohen's house. They all had to be connected somehow.

Joe realized that the electronic device Frank recovered from the crash wreckage had to be a link. Someone who knew that Frank had found the device could have followed him, waiting for the best chance to ambush him and steal it. He or she—whoever it was—knocked Frank out at Scott's garage.

When he didn't find the device on Frank's body, he backtracked to Phil's house. Then he jumped Phil and set the fire to cover his tracks. The fire was so intense that no one could ever be sure if the device had been stolen or destroyed in the blaze.

"Whoever it was," Joe grumbled, "had a very busy day."

Suddenly he froze in his tracks and smacked his forehead with the palm of his hand. "That's it!" he muttered to himself. "It *couldn't* be Scott. He might have a motive for wanting McCoy out of the race—but how could he have known Phil had the gizmo in the first place? Scott couldn't have tailed Frank because he was in his garage with *me* all afternoon."

Joe did an abrupt about-face and started to walk back toward Phil's house, hoping Frank would still be there. He picked up the pace as he turned the problem over in his mind, trying to look at all the angles.

Suddenly he stopped again. There was a small hole in his argument that got larger and larger the more he tried to ignore it—and he knew Frank would see it right away. Joe could just imagine the very short conversation they'd have.

Joe: Scott couldn't have known Phil had the device.

Frank: He could have had an accomplice.

Joe: My gut instinct tells me Scott didn't do it.

Frank: Then ask your gut instinct for a list of other suspects.

Joe shook his head. Sometimes his brother was just *too* logical and rational. Instinct and intuition weren't enough for Frank Hardy.

Joe started walking again. He would just have to come up with a better suspect, he told himself. "Okay, gut instinct," he muttered to himself, "tell me who did it."

There was no answer. Even though Joe sometimes acted without thinking, this was different. This wasn't action, it was just a different kind of thinking—sort of thinking without thinking.

He slammed his fist into a tree and winced with pain and frustration. "Intuition," he concluded out loud, "isn't helping me out right now."

Joe had been walking for some time, not thinking about where he was going. He plunged out into an intersection without even glancing at the traffic light. The blare of a car horn and the squeal of tires snapped him out of his fog, and he leapt back to the curb.

"Watch where you're going, idiot!" someone shouted from a passing car.

Joe looked around and realized he was less than a block from Callie Shaw's house. Callie was Frank's girlfriend and mostly a pain in Joe's neck. "I can't figure that girl out," he grumbled. "Sometimes she does the weirdest—"

Joe suddenly stopped without completing his

thought—because another one had just taken its place. Girls, he thought, are supposed to know a lot about stuff like intuition. Maybe Callie can help me out. He headed for her house.

It was late, but Joe was in luck. Callie was still up, working with her video equipment.

"Get lost on the way to an all-night launder-ette?" Callie quipped as she invited Joe in. "You look like you could use the heavy-duty machine."

Joe looked at himself in the hall mirror. He was a mess. His blond hair had turned brown with dirt and ashes. His face and clothes were grimed with soot, and one sleeve was missing from his shirt.

"And you smell like you've been barbecuing old tires," she said, sniffing.

"Nice to see you, too, Callie," Joe replied. "Making movies of yourself again?"

"Gee, it's fun to stand here and trade insults with you, Joe, but it's kind of late and I've got work to do. Maybe we could make a date to continue this later."

Joe paused a second and then said, "Look, I'm sorry. Let's start over, okay?"

Callie took a closer look at Joe. She could see that something was troubling him. "Okay, Joe," she said. "What can I do for you?"

Joe slumped down and sat on the floor to tell Callie about the events that followed Angus McCoy's fatal crash, concluding with, "I don't have any *proof*—I just have a *feeling*. Know what I mean?''

''Well, this is a switch.'' Callie smiled. ''Are you asking for my *advice*, Joe?''

Joe shrugged. ''Yeah, I guess I am.''

''Guys always make jokes about 'female intuition' and complain that women aren't rational. They don't understand that it's possible to see things from a different angle. Sometimes you have to pay more attention to emotions than physical actions.'' Callie looked up. ''Are you with me so far?''

Joe nodded. ''Yeah, I think so.''

Callie chuckled. ''Sometimes it's better *not* to think. Some things don't have logical explanations.''

''Like my coming here tonight,'' Joe said.

''Well, yes,'' Callie admitted. ''Look, let me put it another way. Scott Lavin is your friend, right?''

''Right.''

''Then if he's guilty, you've got lousy instincts when it comes to picking friends. But I know most of your friends, and I think you have pretty good instincts.

''So, other than Scott Lavin,'' she prodded, ''who has the most to gain—or lose—in this race?''

Joe ran a mental checklist and then said, ''Russell Arno, the race promoter, and Reinhart Voss, the other driver for McCoy Racing. With McCoy out of the way, Voss would be the number-one driver for the team, and he would have a better shot at winning."

"What about Arno?" Callie asked.

"I can't give you a reason," Joe admitted. "I don't know that much about him—or even what a promoter does. I just don't trust the guy."

"Okay," Callie said. "Now, which one does your instinct tell you is the more likely suspect?"

Joe didn't even have to think about it. The answer just popped out. "Arno," he said. "I think he's hiding something."

Callie stood up. "Then let's go check him out," she replied, grabbing her purse and heading for the door.

"Wait a minute!" Joe burst out. "Where do you think you're going? I don't need a girl tagging along."

"Okay." Callie smiled. "I'll go by myself— and I have a car. How were *you* planning to get to his office?"

Joe grinned weakly. "I don't suppose you'd consider giving me a lift?"

"There's not enough room in my car for your macho self-image," Callie chided him. "You'll have to leave it here and pick it up later."

When they got to the Bayport Fairgrounds it was late.

"What'll we do if Arno's not in his office?" Callie asked.

"We'll cross that bridge when we come to it," Joe whispered as they reached the mobile trailer that served as Arno's traveling office.

He walked up the steps and tapped lightly on the door. It was unlocked and creaked open slightly as Joe knocked. He pushed the door open all the way and stuck his head inside. The lights were on, but no one was in sight. "Hello?" he called. "Anybody here?"

Joe cautiously stepped inside. Somebody else had been through the place recently, and he doubted that it was Arno. Papers and file folders were scattered on the floor, along with several drawers that had been yanked out of the desk. Joe whistled softly. "This guy is one lousy housekeeper."

Callie brushed past Joe and started to pick things up and examine them. "We'll call Dial-A-Maid when we're through," she joked, picking up a heap of folders and leafing through them. "We don't even know what we're looking for," she said. "Tell you what, Joe—you look through the files while I watch TV."

Joe noticed a color television in the corner, with a videocassette recorder stacked on top of it. "That VCR looks unusual," he observed.

"Yeah," Callie replied as her hands skimmed over the control panel. "It's a professional model."

Joe sat down in Arno's chair. "Well, I guess that's part of what a promoter does," he said.

"He makes a lot of flashy, full-color videos of fast cars and—"

Joe stopped in midsentence, his eyes riveted to the name typed on the front of one of the file folders on the desk. "Bingo!" he called out. "This one has McCoy's name on it."

Joe opened the folder and shuffled through the papers inside. He kept up a running commentary. "Press releases, pictures of McCoy and his car, a couple of contracts, some canceled checks. It looks like Arno was paying McCoy to appear at races."

Joe turned over one of the checks and looked at the back. Then he flipped over several more. "Mmm—this is strange. McCoy endorsed all of these checks to some outfit called Clarco Industries. But I don't see anything here worth killing him for. . . ."

Joe's voice trailed off as he pulled out one of the documents. The silence drew Callie's attention, and she turned to look at Joe. He wasn't sitting anymore; his feet were planted firmly on the ground, and he was leaning over the desk, reading intently.

"What is it?" Callie asked.

Joe didn't reply. He just kept on reading.

"Come on, Joe," Callie urged. "What *is* it?"

"An insurance policy," he said at last, looking up with a triumphant smile. "A *life* insurance policy for a million bucks."

"So Arno has some life insurance. So what?"

"Arno has some life insurance," Joe repeated. "But not on his own life. This policy pays off on *McCoy's* death!"

Joe jumped up and waved the piece of paper in Callie's face. "Do you know what this means?" he asked excitedly.

Callie didn't say anything. She was staring at something over Joe's shoulder—something in the doorway, Joe realized.

"It means you're in the wrong place at the wrong time," a cold, smooth voice answered.

Chapter

8

JOE HARDY KNEW the voice that had just threatened him, and he didn't like it any more now than he had the first time he heard it. Well, Joe thought, I came here looking for Russell Arno, and now I've found him.

Joe was in a tight spot. He had his back to Arno, and Arno was blocking his only exit. Joe thought about spinning around and trying to take Arno by surprise. That might buy enough time for Callie to get away. But the man could be armed. Joe gritted his teeth and decided to go for it anyway.

I got Callie into this, Joe told himself. It's up to me to get her out.

Callie was looking right at Arno, and she spoke before Joe could act. "Oh, Mr. Arno! Thank heaven you're here!" she exclaimed, clasping her hands together as if she was about to start praying. She was doing her best imitation of a little lost girl. It was almost good enough for an Academy Award, and Joe hoped it was good enough to fool Arno.

"We were just passing by," Callie continued, "when we saw your door was open. We came in to make sure everything was all right. We were afraid something might have happened to you."

Joe was impressed. Callie might just pull this one off. He felt a slight tug on the piece of paper he was still holding in his hand. He looked down and realized that Callie was trying to pry it loose and quietly stuff it in her purse.

Joe shielded her with his body, hiding Callie's actions from Arno's view. He turned to face the promoter as Callie closed her purse with the insurance policy tucked inside.

"So you were taking a little stroll around the fairgrounds at—" Arno paused to glance at his watch. "Not a very convincing story. What do you think, Mr. Hardy?"

"What are *you* doing here this late?" Joe countered.

"That's none of your business," Arno snapped. "But I have nothing to hide. I was in my room at the motel when someone tripped the silent alarm in the office."

"Wait a minute," Joe said. "How did you know the alarm went off?"

"Mobile phone," Arno said simply. "The

alarm here sends a signal to my personal phone. I take it everywhere—a clever device, don't you think?''

"Wouldn't it make more sense to hook up the alarm to notify the police?'' Callie asked.

"It might," Arno admitted. "But I'm on the move a lot, traveling from city to city, following the racing circuit. I'd have to make special arrangements with the police in each city. It's easier this way.''

"So why didn't you call the police?'' Joe persisted.

Arno shrugged. "The motel is closer to here than the police station. I didn't want the burglar— excuse me, *burglars*—to get away before the police arrived.''

Joe reached across the promoter's desk and grabbed the telephone. "Look, Mr. Arno, we're telling you the truth. The place was like this when we got here. But if you don't believe us, let's phone the police right now.'' He was bluffing, and he was betting Arno wouldn't call.

Who would believe that the two of them had just sort of stumbled onto the scene? Joe had already talked his way out of one tight spot that night. If Arno called his bluff—and the cops— things could get very ugly.

Arno moved around the desk and sat down in his chair. His hand rested on the telephone for a moment as he sized up Joe and Callie. Joe's gaze was steady as he returned the man's stare. Go ahead, Joe's eyes dared, make your move.

Finally Arno let go of the phone and moved his hand to his inside coat pocket. "No," he said, "I don't think that will be necessary. But the question is, now that I have you, what do I do with you?"

Now who's bluffing, Joe wondered. Does he have a gun? Joe's whole body went tense, ready to leap across the desk and crash into the promoter at the first glimpse of a concealed weapon.

"I guess you could just shoot us." Joe smiled, raising the stakes. "But that would be too messy, wouldn't it? Too many loose ends. Too many questions."

"What are you talking about?" Arno replied, pulling a pack of cigarettes out of his pocket. "I don't suppose either of you has a light? No, you wouldn't. Nobody does anymore. This is the only place I can smoke without being nagged." He gave them a foul look.

"But we weren't talking about my bad habits, were we? We were talking about murder, I believe. And you were just about to tell me why I would want to shoot you."

"You probably wouldn't," Joe said. "Shooting isn't your style. Accidents are more convenient, aren't they?"

"Ah, that's it," Arno said, laughing. "You and your girlfriend are slinking around playing junior detective. You think Angus McCoy was the victim of foul play, and I'm the closest thing you have to a suspect. You came here looking for evidence and tore the place apart when you couldn't find anything.''

"I told you we didn't ransack your office," Joe snapped. "And I think I have a pretty good idea why you would like to see McCoy dead.'' Joe was tightly gripping the edge of the desk with both hands. He leaned over to look directly into Arno's face—and accidentally pushed one of the file folders onto the floor.

It landed with a soft plop, and Joe glanced down at the noise. Nice move, Joe, he said to himself. Brilliant timing.

The label on the file read: "McCoy, Angus.''

A hand reached down and picked up the folder. "Find any worthwhile reading in here?'' Arno asked, opening the file and sorting through the contents.

"We weren't looking for anything," Callie insisted. "We were just—''

"I know, I know," Arno interrupted. "You were just passing by." He took a key ring out of his coat pocket and unlocked the top desk drawer. He casually pulled out a gun and leveled it at Callie. "And I'm sure you're both quite anxious to leave. But would you mind if I search you before you go? Something seems to be missing, and I don't like it when people walk off with my property.''

Joe mentally kicked himself. He had let Arno's slick routine lull him into letting down his guard.

Callie opened her purse slowly. "There's no need for that, Mr. Arno," she said, removing the crumpled insurance policy. "I think this is what you're looking for."

The promoter reached for the document with his free hand, but Callie let go of the paper just before he grasped it, and it fluttered to the floor. Arno stooped down to pick it up, and his aim wavered slightly.

Joe moved like lightning. Still clutching the edge of the desk, he heaved it up and over on top of Arno. Then he slammed all his weight into it, pinning the man down.

"Oof!" the promoter grunted as the weapon flew out of his hand and skittered across the floor.

"Grab the gun!" Joe shouted to Callie.

"Ugh," Callie replied, carefully lifting the automatic pistol. "I hate these things."

She looked at Joe. "Now what?"

"I'll hold him while you call the police," Joe said.

"Great idea," Callie said. "Where's the phone?"

"Down here," a muffled voice came from underneath the overturned desk. "I'd make the call myself if the thing were still working. I guess it wasn't designed to have large pieces of furniture dropped on it. Come to think of it," Arno groaned, "neither was I. How about letting me out from under here? I think we can clear up this whole misunderstanding."

"Only after you hand me that insurance policy," Joe demanded.

Arno stuck out his hand and waved the document like a white flag of surrender. Joe snatched it away and handed it to Callie. He dragged the desk off Arno and said, "Okay, you can get up now—but *slowly*."

Arno grabbed on to a leg of the toppled desk and hauled himself up. "That insurance policy doesn't prove anything," he said. "It's common business practice. McCoy was my star attraction. The deals I make with cities like Bayport guarantee that McCoy will be there for the race. Without McCoy, I could lose a lot of money."

"So why'd you pull a gun on us?" Joe asked roughly.

"Look, kid," the promoter snapped. "I'm getting tired of your questions. You say you didn't break in here. You say you were just passing by and found my office this way. I'll take your word for it—but don't press your luck."

He glared at them. "Now get out of here before I change my mind—and leave the policy and the gun here. It would be real unfortunate if the police found you with a stolen firearm."

Joe took the document and the pistol from Callie. He deftly removed the clip and cleared the chamber, ejecting the bullet that had been loaded and ready to fire. "You go ahead, Callie," he said. "I'll be out in a minute."

He handed the piece of paper to Arno and tossed the unloaded weapon into the farthest corner of the office. "You be real careful where you aim that thing," Joe said as he stormed out the door. "Next time I might just make you *eat* it."

"I still don't trust him," Joe muttered to Callie as they walked away. "But I don't have any evidence!"

"You ever wonder why girls always lug around big, heavy purses wherever they go?" Callie asked.

"Huh?" Joe frowned. "What's that got to do with—"

"It's just in case they come across some evidence," Callie grinned, reaching into her handbag and pulling out a videocassette. "While you were reading files, I was reading tape labels. Check this one out."

Joe squinted in the dark trying to read the handwritten scrawl on the side of the plastic case. He stopped under a streetlight and held up the cassette to catch the light. " 'Master tape,' " he read aloud. " 'Angus McCoy Bayport Grand Prix Time Trial.' "

"Maybe this is what whoever broke into Arno's office was looking for," Joe mused. "But why didn't they take it?"

"Because they couldn't find it," Callie answered. "It wasn't on the shelves with the other tapes. It was in the VCR."

Joe just stared at Callie. "I can't believe it," he said. "Frank and I have both been so busy trying to unearth clues that we forgot Arno had the whole thing on videotape!"

Chapter

9

IT WAS ALMOST noon the next day before Joe Hardy stumbled out of bed and staggered downstairs, looking for his brother. Joe hadn't meant to oversleep, but it had been a long night.

Frank wasn't anywhere in sight. Only his aunt Gertrude was home, puttering in the garden.

"Is Frank around?" Joe asked. "There's something I want to show him."

"You just missed him," Gertrude said, looking up from her tomato plants. "Callie picked him up a while ago, and they drove over to the hospital to see that nice Cohen boy. Poor thing. Did you hear what happened to him last night?"

"Yeah, I kind of heard something about it," Joe said evasively. If his aunt ever found out that Frank and he had almost gotten killed saving Phil

73

Cohen from the fire, she'd have a heart attack on the spot.

"I think I'll go over to the hospital, too," Joe told his aunt. He dug in his hip pocket, fished out the keys to the van, and loped across the lawn to the driveway.

"Oh, that reminds me," Gertrude called after him. "Your brother told me to tell you to take the van and meet him at the hospital."

Joe turned and smiled at her. "Say, Aunt Gertrude, you know what I think I'll do?"

"What?"

"I think I'll take the van and meet Frank at the hospital."

"You do that," she said, nodding as she plucked a ripe tomato and dropped it into her basket.

Joe drove to the hospital by the fastest route. He wanted to make sure Phil was okay—and he was anxious to talk with his brother.

When Joe got there, he found Phil sitting up in bed, talking with Frank and Callie.

"Come on in, Joe," Phil greeted him. "Your brother tells me you saved my life. I guess I owe you one."

"I had a little help," Joe replied, looking right at Frank.

"Hey, what are brothers for?" Frank said.

"Look, Frank," Joe started, "I'm sorry—"

"No, *I'm* sorry," Frank interrupted. "We both said some things we really didn't mean, but at least you had a reason. Scott's your friend, and maybe I should have checked out all the other leads before pointing my finger at him.

"Well, I'm beginning to have my doubts, too," Joe admitted. "I haven't exactly done a tremendous job of digging up evidence that will stick to any other suspects. I thought I had something on Arno, but that guy's got an answer for everything."

"We were lucky he didn't have us arrested for assault," Callie added.

Phil coughed and said, "That reminds me. It took me a long time to go over that electronic device that seems to be so popular with the assault and arson set."

"Did you find out anything?" Frank asked.

"Hard to say for sure. The circuitry was too complex for a simple remote triggering device. So if you were thinking it was some kind of detonator for a small explosive or something, you'll have to think again."

Phil shrugged. "I could probably tell you more if I had whatever it was connected to."

"Then I guess that's what we'll have to find," Joe said. "I wanted to do a little swimming before the end of the season, anyway. How about you?" he added, nudging his brother. "Last one in is a rotten diver."

"Wait a second," Callie protested. "Before you both go leap into the bay and get sucked out to sea by the tides, how about watching a fascinating documentary over at my house?''

Joe slapped his forehead, realizing he had forgotten to tell his brother about the videocassette. That was what he wanted to talk to Frank about in the first place.

"That's okay," Frank said before Joe could open his mouth. "Callie told me all about your little adventure last night. I just can't let the two of you go *anywhere* without me, can I?"

Frank Hardy clapped his brother on the back and laughed. Then his tone shifted. "From now on," he spoke seriously, "we stick together wherever the trail leads. Agreed?"

"We both get in too much trouble alone." Joe chuckled and grasped his brother's outstretched right hand. "Agreed."

Joe and Frank decided to take a detour past the Bayport Fairgrounds, so they told Callie they'd meet her at her house.

"Why don't we check out Reinhart Voss," Joe suggested. "With McCoy gone, he'll get the whole team effort for the race. I don't think that's enough to make him kill the guy, but it's a start."

"Maybe he was tired of racing in McCoy's shadow," Frank ventured as he pulled the van into a parking space near the Bayport Motel, the closest spot they could park to the fairgrounds.

"Yeah," Joe said, opening the van door and jumping out. "And maybe he trashed Scott's engine to have an even better shot at winning the race.''

They walked to the fairgrounds. Fuel and exhaust fumes drifted through the air. The entire grounds had been transformed into a giant outdoor garage, bustling with activity.

They passed one of the sheds where a Formula One engine was being revved up. The noise was deafening. ''I guess mufflers are optional on these things!'' Frank yelled.

They found Voss with his head mechanic, making some last-minute adjustments to his car for his final time-trial run.

''Is it not a beautiful thing?'' The German driver smiled broadly, gesturing with both hands to indicate his 900-horsepower pride and joy. ''You are just in time to watch me get the pole position with the fastest qualifying time!''

Joe stooped down and ran his hand over the smooth, sleek surface of the car. It was contoured to cut through the wind like a knife. ''With McCoy gone and Scott Lavin's engine damaged,'' he began casually, ''I guess you're feeling pretty confident.''

Voss's smile quickly faded. ''I learned much from Angus,'' he said quietly. ''I will miss him— and I will also miss the chance to beat him. It is good to win, but better to win against the best.''

''Do you really think you could have beaten him?'' Frank asked.

''He was getting old,'' Voss replied bluntly.

"Maybe I would not have beaten him here. But next year I drive for Ferrari."

"You're leaving McCoy Racing?" Joe cut in.

"Yes," Voss said. "As long as I stayed with Angus I would have been number two, always getting the second-best equipment. So when Ferrari offered me their number-one slot, I jumped. This is my last race for McCoy. Maybe I can leave the team with a small victory. It should not be too hard."

Frank gave him a puzzled look. "What do you mean?"

"This is an exhibition race," Voss explained. "Most teams are here just to test out new equipment. Some of the top drivers are not even here. This is the kind of race that gives the younger drivers a chance."

"Like Scott Lavin?" Frank suggested.

"Why, yes," Voss agreed. "A win here would look very good for Scott."

The Hardys looked at each other as the German driver climbed into the cockpit of his car and put on his crash helmet. Joe knew what Frank was thinking.

The powerful engine roared to life, and Frank put his fingers in his ears. Joe leaned into the cockpit and tapped the top of the driver's helmet. Voss flipped up the visor and cocked his head in Joe's direction. Joe cupped his hands around his mouth and shouted, "But Scott's out of the race, right? His engine's no good!"

In response, Voss shrugged his shoulders in the confined space and jerked his right thumb over his shoulder, pointing behind him. Then he punched the accelerator, the tires screamed and smoked in protest, and the race car swerved out onto the roadway and took off down the course.

Joe and Frank both turned in the direction Voss had pointed and saw the familiar yellow-and-red Formula One barreling down the course, heading straight at them.

The Hardys jumped back as Scott Lavin's car screeched to a halt right next to them. Scott was laughing as he took off his helmet. He shut down the engine and squirmed out of the cockpit, handing the crash helmet to Joe as he climbed over the side of the car.

"We're back in the race, Joe!" Scott exclaimed. "When I got the police call and came down to the garage last night, I thought it was all over. But we worked all night and half the morning to fix the engine."

Joe was staring at the ground, his hands stuffed in his hip pockets, waiting for the bomb to drop. The police report would have put Frank and Joe at the scene, and Scott was bound to want some answers. Joe swallowed hard. "About last night," he began.

"If it weren't for you guys," Scott interrupted, "we never could have pulled it off."

"Huh?" Joe mumbled. Frank kicked him, signaling him to shut up.

"I don't know how you did it, but a cop named Riley said you guys reported the break-in and chased off whoever did it before he could do any real damage.

"Anyway," Scott continued, starting to climb back into the race car, "I just wanted to say thanks." He paused with one leg in the cockpit and the other on the ground. Then he looked at Joe and said, "Say, since you're already holding the helmet, why don't you put it on and drive this baby back to the shed?"

Joe's mouth dropped open. He could barely believe what he was hearing. Ever since he could remember, he had loved cars. He was the first person in line to get his driver's license. It seemed he had waited half his life for it. Now he was actually getting a chance to drive the ultimate racing machine.

But as badly as Joe wanted to get behind the wheel, he remembered his promise to his brother. They had agreed to stick together, and Joe wasn't about to let a car come between Frank and him. "Thanks, anyway, Scott," Joe said, shaking his head. "But I don't think so. We've got stuff to do."

Frank knew that it took a lot of willpower for Joe to decline Scott's offer, and he was proud of him. "Oh, go ahead," he urged his brother. "I'll meet you back at the van. I want to see if I can find that writer, T. B. Martin, and ask him a few more questions."

Joe didn't need any more encouragement. He put one hand on the roll bar and the other on the wind screen, stepped into the cockpit, and slid down into the seat. Scott reached in and grabbed the metal catch-plate attached to the "antisubmarine" straps—the straps that come up between the driver's legs. Then he helped Joe buckle in the two shoulder harnesses and both ends of the lap belt. The catch-plate connected all the straps together, like a six-pointed star, right over Joe's navel.

Joe shifted his weight around to get comfortable in the half-sitting, half-lying position and stared at the dizzying array of controls. "How come all these gauges are tilted?" he asked.

"We rotate them," Scott pointed out, "so the needles point straight up at optimum levels."

"Okay." Joe nodded, scanning the dials. "I think I've got it." But something was missing. "Hey," he said, frowning, "Where's the speedometer?"

Scott laughed. "The only speed we worry about is the other guy's. If he's going faster than you are, then you aren't going fast enough. But today let's take it nice and slow," Scott cautioned. "These monsters aren't exactly designed for idling. If you let your RPMs drop too low, she'll stall. So you'll have to kind of roll your right foot between the brake and the accelerator, braking and revving the engine at the same time. Got it?"

"Uh-huh." Joe nodded eagerly. "Here goes nothing."

Joe pushed in the clutch with his left foot, gripped the stick shift with his right hand, and shoved it into the first-gear position. With his right foot on the gas pedal, he watched the tachometer needle jump as he revved the engine. Then he eased his left foot off the clutch, and the car lurched into gear.

Frank saw his brother give him a thumbs-up as he steered the race car onto the road. Scott Lavin turned to him and said, "He's pretty good. Most guys stall out the first time they get behind the wheel."

"Joe's a fast learner," Frank replied. He started to walk away but turned back when he heard a shout rise up from the small cluster of spectators. Looking around to see what had caused the commotion, Frank saw a few people standing up, pointing down the road.

A black cloud began to billow over the race course. The trail of acrid smoke led down to a burning vehicle, and Frank could see that it was the same color as the flames that engulfed it—yellow and red.

Horror crept up on Frank as he realized slowly it was Scott's car and Joe was still in it!

Chapter

10

JOE HARDY HAD just been starting to get the feel of the race car when he heard a muffled explosion over the loud thrum of the engine behind him. His eyes darted from one side mirror to the other, and both showed him the same thing—billowing smoke and flame.

Joe didn't panic. He slammed on the brakes, reached down with his right hand, and hit the fire extinguisher release switch. Within seconds, he knew, the cockpit would be sprayed with a layer of fire-retardant chemicals, giving him time to get out safely.

But nothing happened.

He hit the switch again. Still nothing. "Great," he muttered. "No protective clothes, no fire extinguisher—and no time! I've got to get out now or I'll end up the main course at a surprise cookout!"

Joe slapped the release button on the restraint straps, threw the shoulder harness back over his head, and grabbed the lip of the cockpit to haul himself out. "Yarrghh!" he screamed in pain, wrenching his hands away from the searing hot metal.

He was trapped! He was wedged so tightly in the tiny space that he couldn't move without using his hands and arms for leverage. "No pain, no gain." He grimaced, psyching himself up to take hold of the burning metal and pull himself free.

Joe reached out with both hands—and felt a cool mist pour down on him.

Frank sprinted into the nearest shed and grabbed a fire extinguisher off the wall. Then he rushed back out and starting running toward the burning car. He caught up with Scott Lavin, who was headed in the same direction.

"He'll be all right," Scott huffed, trying to keep up with Frank's desperate pace. "There's an on-board fire extinguisher."

"I'm not taking any chances!" Frank yelled. A small knot of onlookers blocked his way. He shoved his way through the crowd, swinging the fire extinguisher to clear a path. "Out of the way!" he bellowed. "Coming through!"

Frank emptied the fire extinguisher into the

cockpit of the burning machine and tossed the canister aside. He grabbed Joe's arms, yanking him out with one tremendous heave. The two brothers tumbled away from the blaze.

The small crowd that had gathered at the scene quickly scattered as an ambulance and a fire engine rolled up. The fire fighters jumped off the truck, and within seconds the blaze was out, leaving nothing but a cloud of smoke and steam—and a smouldering heap where a high-performance race car had been a moment before.

Frank helped Joe to his feet, then looked at the burned-out hulk that had been Scott Lavin's first and only Formula One car. He glimpsed Scott standing off to one side, staring in wide-eyed disbelief, his dream disappearing in a cloud of smoke.

Joe turned his gaze to his brother. "We've got to find out who's behind this before anybody else gets killed," he said grimly.

Frank and Joe showed up at Callie Shaw's house about two hours late. "You guys always seem to think that the shortest distance between two points involves two or three stops in between," she commented after hearing the story. "Does this mean you've whittled your list of suspects down to none?"

"Well, you have to admit," Joe said, "that Scott Lavin would have to be pretty desperate to blow up his own race car."

"We need more facts," Frank replied. "Maybe the videotape of McCoy's crash will tell us something."

"I still don't see why we couldn't watch it on our own VCR at home," Joe protested as they followed Callie through the house.

"I told you," Callie said. "Mine is a *professional* video cassette like Arno's. It uses wider tape than home models. The cassette wouldn't even fit in the slot on your machine." She led the way down the basement stairs.

"My folks let me use the den down here for my video equipment," Callie said. "I've got a professional-format VCR hooked up to the wide-screen TV." She took the videocassette over to a large, black box with an imposing set of knobs and dials on the front and a maze of wires snaking out the back. She pushed the cassette through a slot in the machine. "It's show time!" she announced.

Frank pulled over some folding directors' chairs, and they all sat down to watch. "Just fast forward to the part where McCoy goes through the tunnel," Frank said.

Callie pressed a button and the action flew across the screen at a breakneck speed. Joe remembered how, looking down on the scene from the air, McCoy's car hadn't seemed to be moving very fast. Now it was comical the way it whizzed down the course and darted around the turns. "Is that some kind of digital clock?" he asked, pointing to a row of changing numbers at the bottom of the screen.

"Yes," Callie said. "Video master tapes have a time code for editing purposes. It keeps precise track of the time down to hundredths of seconds."

"Here it comes," Frank cut in, staring intently as the race car entered the dark mouth of the tunnel. "Slow it down now."

Callie pressed another button, and the tape slowed to normal speed. The digital clock slowed down, too. The Hardys watched as the car disappeared inside and the helicopter swung out over the ocean to record the scene from the exit point of the tunnel.

"Hold it right there!" Frank commanded. "Now play it in slow motion." They could see the low-slung profile of the race car as it gradually emerged from the tunnel. "It's hard to tell from this angle," Frank noted, "but it looks like he's weaving a little."

"Like he lost control *before* he hit the turn," Joe said. "And it seems like he's awfully low in the cockpit. You can barely see the top of his helmet."

"Like he was unconscious and slumped over?" Frank suggested.

The videotape kept rolling in slow motion, and they watched the race car push out the guardrail as if it were sliding through a wall of butter. "I wish we had a better camera angle," Frank muttered.

The car rolled slightly to one side as it fell toward the water. "Now you can't see him at all!" he complained.

"Great shot of the axles, though," Joe said, trying to joke.

As gruesome as it was, they replayed the scene several times, looking for anything they might have missed. "Okay, Callie," Frank finally said. "You can shut it off. This isn't going to tell us enough."

"Looks like it's time to go diving," Joe said.

"Looks that way," Frank agreed.

They left the videocassette with Callie and headed home to pick up some equipment. "The scuba gear's loaded in back," Joe said as he climbed into the van's passenger seat.

"Good," Frank replied. He was already behind the wheel, and the engine was running. "Then let's get going." He backed the van out of the driveway and headed down the street.

When they got to the end of the block, Frank turned left. "Hey, this isn't the way to the marina!" Joe protested. "Aren't we going to take the boat?"

Frank smiled. "I thought we'd take the scenic route."

Joe glanced at Frank and knew he wasn't going to get any more information out of him. So Joe bided his time reading the street signs and trying to second-guess his older brother.

After a few minutes Joe said, "Frank, I think you just made a wrong turn. This road leads to—"

"I know," Frank nodded. "You want to take a look at McCoy's car, and I want to take another look at the crash site." He turned the wheel sharply and the van swerved onto an old dirt road.

They bumped along the twin ruts for a couple miles, until they came in sight of Barmet Bay. "I'd forgotten about this old access road," Joe said as he opened the back door of the van and started to take out the scuba gear.

"Good thing I didn't," Frank said, hoisting a coil of thick rope. "With the highway blocked off for the race, we would have had a long walk."

Frank crouched down to look at something. "What is it?" Joe asked.

"It looks like someone else has been here recently," Frank replied, running his hand along the ground. "Footprints."

Joe shrugged. "Probably somebody came up for the view. Come on. Let's get moving."

The two brothers clambered down a steep incline to the paved road that skirted the cliff. They then followed the road around the hairpin turn. Joe stopped by a pair of wooden barriers with flashing emergency lights bolted to them. They were blocking the ragged gash in the guardrail where McCoy had crashed.

Frank kept walking all the way to the tunnel, scanning the roadway as he went. "Just as I thought!" he shouted. "There aren't any skid marks!" He trotted back to where Joe was standing. "Do you know what that means?"

"Yeah," Joe nodded. "Either he didn't even hit the brakes or nothing happened when he did. He just plowed over the edge without slowing down."

"And that means it definitely wasn't an accident," Frank added, moving around the saw-horses.

"You'd think someone like Arno or the police would have noticed that," Joe said.

Frank shrugged. "They had already decided it *was* an accident. They weren't really looking for anything else."

He motioned to Joe. "It looks like we can climb down most of the way without using the rope."

"Then what?" Joe asked.

"Then you put on the scuba gear and I lower you down into the water."

"Why don't I lower *you* down?" Joe suggested hopefully, slinging the bulky air tank over his shoulder. He didn't care much for the idea of rappeling down the cliff in a wet suit with that thing on his back and flippers on his feet.

"Because that's not part of my plan," Frank insisted. "If you don't like it, you can think up the plan next time."

They worked their way down to a rather large

ledge with a single scraggly tree that grew up against the cliff. Frank lashed the rope to the tree trunk to support Joe's weight while Joe put on the scuba gear. He double-checked the pressure in the tank, ran his hand over the air hose, and tested the regulator by breathing through it to make sure he was getting air from the tank.

"Okay, I'm ready," Joe announced when he was sure everything was in working order.

Frank tied the other end of the rope around Joe's chest, under his armpits. Then Frank took a firm stance with his legs wide apart and his knees slightly bent. Standing with his back to the tree, he wound the rope once around each of his arms and gripped the line tightly.

"I'll do most of the work," he explained. "I'll let out the rope slowly. The tree will be a backup to hold you. You just keep yourself away from the cliff wall."

Joe gave a tug on the line and then leaned backward over the edge. "Everybody into the pool!" he yelled, and pushed off with both feet.

It worked perfectly. Joe relaxed a little as he inched downward. When he was close to the water line, he gave a firm shove with both feet, pushing himself out to clear a jumble of rocks at the bottom of the cliff. But suddenly the line went slack, and he splashed into the cold Atlantic, gasping and spluttering for air.

The force of the fall had ripped the regulator from his mouth. A few swift kicks brought him back to the surface. "Nice going, ace!" he shouted up at his brother.

There was no response. From this angle, Joe couldn't see the tree, the ledge, or Frank. He ducked underwater for a moment to wriggle out of the rope.

Joe popped back up again and yanked off his face mask. He looked up again. He thought he caught a glimmer of movement, but he couldn't be sure. He was just about to shout again when he saw something hurtling over the side of the ledge.

It was Frank—his arms and legs flailing—plummeting toward the rocks!

Chapter

11

FRANK HIT the water hard, barely missing the rocks jutting out from the foot of the cliff. Stunned by the impact, he sank deeper and deeper beneath the waves into an engulfing darkness.

At last, the cold, salty wetness woke him. At first he didn't know where he was or how he got there. I was standing on the edge of the cliff, he recalled. Then I was in the air, and now I'm underwater—with my hands tied behind my back!

He thrashed around and discovered that his hands weren't really tied. He was just tangled up in the climbing rope. Frank unwound the rope and let it drift away from him. Then he kicked his way upward. His head broke the surface, and he greedily gulped in fresh air.

Frank started to tread water and looked around

to get his bearings. Suddenly someone loomed out of the water right in front of him, startling him.

"Take it easy! It's only me," Joe exclaimed, pushing the diving mask up over his forehead. "Are you okay? That looked like a vicious fall."

"Yeah," Frank said, wiping the hair out of his eyes. "If this were the Olympics, it would have been a perfect 0.0 dive."

"What happened?" Joe asked. "Did the rope break?"

"It had to have been cut back by the tree," Frank stated flatly.

"What?"

"I did a nosedive into the dirt on the ledge," Frank said. "I thought the tree must have snapped or something."

"So what changed your mind?"

"Well, there I was, starting to get back up and feeling pretty proud of myself for keeping hold of the rope—when somebody sneaked up behind me and gave me a nice, hard shove over the edge."

"Well, whoever it was is gone now," Joe remarked, squinting up the face of the cliff.

"I think we can get back up by climbing that rockfall," Frank said, pointing to a spot where the cliff had collapsed and a jumble of boulders sloped into the ocean. "I'll swim over and check it out."

He started swimming but looked back over his

shoulder. "You might as well dive down to the wreck and see if you can find anything."

"You read my mind, brother." Joe smiled, slipping the diving mask back down over his eyes and nose. He glanced at his diving watch and said, "See you in thirty." Then he slipped under the waves and was gone.

It was a short, easy swim to the rock fall. Frank was just pulling himself out of the water, thinking about how nice it would be to let his clothes dry off in the sun, when he heard the faint whine of an outboard motor. He turned to see a boat approaching from the direction of the Bayport Marina. Tracing a line from its wake, Frank could see that it was headed straight for the floating marker, bobbing up and down in the swells, that the police divers had attached to McCoy's sunken race car.

Frank lay flat on his stomach and crawled around a large boulder. Whoever it was, Frank wasn't ready to announce his own presence. He hoped his brother was alert enough to notice the oncoming motorboat—and patient enough to stay out of sight and wait for the intruder to make a move.

Joe sighted the wreckage lying upside down on the ocean floor, the wheels turning slowly in the deep currents. Like it doesn't know it's not going anywhere, Joe reflected as he closed in on the object, his legs pumping up and down, beating a steady rhythm through the water.

He enjoyed the silent solitude of the sea. It gave him a chance to let his mind wander. So he was annoyed when he heard the muffled churning of a propeller disturbing the water nearby. He stopped kicking and hovered a few feet above the bottom. Looking up, he could see the sunlight reflecting on the surface and the hull of a boat cutting a wake through the water.

The boat stopped directly above the wreck site, and Joe watched as an anchor sank rapidly, trailing air bubbles as it fell. Instinctively, Joe held his breath so that he wouldn't leave a telltale path of air bubbles. He looked around, veered away from his original course, and glided down behind an outcropping of rock.

A school of fish feeding on the surrounding plants stirred up the water, allowing Joe to breathe again without being detected. Then he waited, knowing what would come next.

Sure enough, after a few minutes, something else splashed through the surface and descended toward the overturned race car. It was a diver. It could even be somebody I know, Joe thought. But with the wet suit and diving mask, I can't see his face or even the color of his hair!

Joe let the current gently push him to the other side of the outcropping so he could get a better look at the diver. He was moving slowly along the under side of the vehicle, brushing his hands over all the mechanical parts. Like he's looking for something he dropped, Joe thought. Or something he doesn't want anybody else to find.

The diver finished his inspection of the exposed drive shaft and axles. But Joe didn't see him remove anything. Then the man—or woman— ducked under the wreck and wriggled, head first, into the cockpit. The ocean carried the sound of metal banging on metal back to Joe's ears, and the diver soon reemerged. Now Joe could clearly see that he was holding something in his left hand.

With his right hand, the mystery diver sheathed the knife he used to pry the thing loose. He floated in the water for a moment and then pushed off from the submerged race car and shot straight up toward the waiting motorboat.

Joe burst from his hiding place, swimming furiously after the diver. If he doesn't see me, Joe prayed, I can catch him by surprise and grab the evidence.

Joe could see that he was too far behind. The diver would reach the surface—and the safety of his boat—before Joe got there. But there wasn't any choice. Got to go for it, Joe urged himself.

Joe kicked as hard as he could and reached the line that attached the anchor to the vessel above. He gripped it firmly and started hauling himself up, hand over hand. Added to the powerful motion of his legs, the straining muscles in his arms helped him gain on the unknown diver.

Joe kept his eyes fixed on his objective as he

closed the distance. But he could see that the man had reached the surface and was starting to climb into his boat.

With a final burst of energy and a desperate lunge, Joe grabbed a flippered foot and dragged the diver back in the water.

It didn't go exactly as Joe had planned. The diver fell on top of him, jostling Joe's face mask loose. Salt water filled the mask, stinging his eyes and making it hard to see.

Joe's only advantage was that the guy didn't know what had hit him. Joe knew he had to take him out fast and hard.

Joe reached out and ripped off the diver's face mask. At least now we'll be even, he thought. And I can see who you are. But the other man was flailing around so much that air bubbles filled the water and made it impossible to see the man's face.

Joe hit the diver in the stomach with both feet as hard as he could. Even though the water slowed his kick, he was able to double the man over. Joe used the kicking motion to push himself away so he could get a better angle of attack, but the move put him above his opponent.

Joe knew that underwater pressure made it easier to move up rather than down. Brilliant tactics, bozo, Joe chided himself. Now the Creature from the Black Lagoon has the advantage! He can come at me faster than I can make a move on him.

As if he could read Joe's mind, the diver suddenly lunged upward, his right arm stabbing through the water. Joe caught a glint of metal. Too late, he realized it was the knife the man had used earlier.

Joe knew he couldn't move fast enough to dodge the blade. He twisted sharply to avoid the fatal blow, and grimaced, waiting for the painful bite of cold steel. But the diver's arm swung away from Joe's body to sever his air hose.

While Joe struggled to the surface for air, the mystery diver made his escape. Joe got a good look only at the motorboat as it sped away from the scene. It was not a welcome sight.

Exhausted by the time he made it back to the rocks, Joe gladly accepted a helping hand from his brother. "I saw the diver go into the water," Frank said, helping Joe take off the scuba tank. "A little later I saw him again, starting to climb back aboard his boat. Then suddenly he kind of flopped back into the water."

Frank shook his head. "You guys were making more commotion than a breaching humpback whale. You probably ruined the fishing for miles around."

Frank paused for a second when Joe shot him a look that could incinerate.

"After that," he continued after a beat, "the next thing I saw was you popping up some distance away from the boat. The other guy surfaced next to it, got in, and bugged out.''

Joe filled Frank in on the missing details. "Whatever it was we thought we'd find on that wreck," he said, "just sailed off into the sunset."

Frank nodded. "If he wasn't holding the device when you hauled him back into the water, he must have dropped it on the deck first. I don't suppose you got a good look at it?''

Joe shook his head.

"Okay," Frank persisted. "How about the guy? What did he look like?''

"It all happened too fast," Joe said, "and we were both wearing diving gear. I didn't get a good look at him.''

Frank scowled.

"But I didn't have to," Joe added. "I got a good look at his boat, and I recognized *it*.''

"Well?" Frank prodded.

Joe Hardy sighed. "The boat belongs to Scott Lavin.''

Chapter

12

FRANK AND JOE scrambled over the rockfall and edged their way along a narrow path back to the ledge where the other half of the climbing rope was still tied to the tree.

"Just as I thought," Frank said, cradling the rope in his hands and holding out the end for Joe to see. "No frays or anything like that. The rope didn't break. It's a clean cut."

"It looks like you were right all along," Joe replied. "Somebody wants to win this race badly enough to kill for it."

"Yeah," Frank agreed. "It seems like a miracle we're still alive." He clapped Joe on the shoulder and turned his head to study the twisted route they'd have to climb to get back to the road above.

Joe followed his brother's gaze. He laughed

softly, shook his head, and said, "I'm glad this was *your* plan, not mine."

"Why's that?"

Joe unslung the scuba tank from his back and thrust it into Frank's arms. "Because it means *you* get to lug this stuff back to the van."

"Hey, hold on a sec—" Frank started to protest.

"No, no," Joe insisted. "I'm sure I heard you say that was part of your plan. The best part, I think."

The Hardys were bone tired by the time they dragged themselves back to the van. "Let's go home," Joe suggested, slouching down in the passenger seat and resting his feet on the dashboard. "I'll sleep; you drive."

"Remember what Callie said," Frank replied, shifting into gear and pulling hard on the steering wheel, spinning the van around on the dirt track. "The shortest distance between two points always involves a couple of stops along the way."

"I'm too wiped out to remember anything," Joe mumbled, closing his eyes and pretending to sleep as they bumped back down the road. "But I think I can guess where we're headed. Let me take a shot in the dark."

"Fire away!" Frank said.

"We're going to the marina to see if we can catch Scott Lavin there."

"Yes and no."

"Huh?"

"Yes, we're headed for the marina, but there's not much chance of running into Scott there. He had a big head start on us."

"Oh, right." Joe nodded. "We're going there to take a pleasure cruise."

"No," Frank said, flicking the turn signal and pulling into the entrance of the Bayport Marina. "We're here to see if anybody saw Scott take his boat out."

"Why? It didn't go out by itself."

"No—but you said you didn't get a good look at the diver. We have to make sure it was Scott and not somebody else in his boat."

They pulled into a parking space and got out of the van. Frank strode over to a small building. A sign over the door read Harbor Master.

As he reached for the doorknob, Joe caught up and put a hand on his shoulder. Pointing down the dock to one of the motorboats moored there, he said, "If someone stole Scott's boat, they were nice enough to return it."

"Hey, whose side are you on, anyway?" Frank asked. "I thought Scott was your friend."

"He *was*," Joe replied sullenly, "until he tried to kill me."

"But he *didn't* try to kill you," Frank pointed out. "He had a chance, and all he did was cut your air hose."

"So what does that prove?" Joe demanded.

"I don't know." Frank shrugged, opening the

door to the small office and waving his brother inside. "Humor me for a while."

The harbor master was a grizzled old guy with a white admiral's cap perched on his wispy hair. "Old sailors never die," Joe whispered. "They just get desk jobs."

"What can I do for you youngsters?" the man asked in a friendly tone.

"We were supposed to meet Scott Lavin here." Frank smiled. "Have you seen him today?"

"That I have," came the reply.

"Really? How long ago?" Joe cut in.

"Let's just check the log," the harbor master said, turning to a large book on the desk behind the counter. "It's all here, you know."

"Does the log say when he took his boat out and when he came back?" Frank asked.

"That it does." The old man nodded. "Wrote it down myself, don't you know. Ah, here it is. See for yourself." The self-styled admiral staggered under the weight of the huge volume as he brought it over and set it on the counter.

Joe and Frank both studied the most recent entries in the log. "Well, that does it," Joe said. "The times fit perfectly."

They thanked the harbor master and walked back to the van in silence. Joe was downcast, Frank lost in thought.

As they drove home, Joe finally said, "It looks like you were right about Scott from the start.

Boy, was I a pinhead. He *used* me. He probably even rigged that engine fire and set me up to be the toasted marshmallow.''

''Possibly,'' Frank said, nodding. ''He could have thrown away his chances of winning the race and torched his own car to throw us off the trail.''

Joe nodded. ''Yeah. It sure beats a murder rap—and when he saw me at the race course, he figured it was better to risk my life than his own.''

''It's *possible*,'' Frank repeated as he turned the van into their driveway. ''But it doesn't do much for me,'' he said as he switched off the ignition and killed the engine.

He opened the door and hopped out of the van without saying anything else. Joe followed him around to the back of the van. ''What do you mean?'' he asked as his brother opened the rear door and started piling gear into Joe's arms.

Frank stopped unloading and turned to look at Joe. ''Think about it.''

''We know Scott was the diver who took something off the wreck. We know when he left the harbor and when he returned.''

''So?'' Joe retorted.

''So who was up on the ledge cutting our climbing rope?'' Frank turned away and walked toward the house. Opening the front door, he called back over his shoulder, ''Are you coming or not? I don't know about you, but I'm exhausted. I'm going inside.''

Joe stared at the pile of gear in his arms. "Aren't you going to help me with this stuff?"

"Sure—I'm holding the door open for you." Frank smiled. "It's all part of my plan."

Joe groaned. "Next time I'm definitely coming up with my own plan." Lugging the scuba gear into the house, he said, "Scott could have had a little help. An accomplice."

Frank started to climb the stairs. "I might have bought that two days ago," he said. "But not now."

"How come?"

"Scott didn't know we were checking things out until the day after McCoy's crash."

"So?"

"Somebody's been following us, dogging our every move since I first picked up that electronic souvenir." Frank pushed open the door to his room.

"Maybe Arno told Scott that you found something," Joe suggested.

"Maybe. But I don't think so."

"Why not?"

Frank smiled again. "Call it a hunch—gut instinct."

Joe chuckled. "Okay, you've got me there. But why did Scott dive down to the wreck and rip off evidence?"

"Beats me." Frank shrugged. "When we find him, we'll ask him."

As if in answer to Frank's statement, they

heard their aunt Gertrude calling, "Boys? Are you up there? You have a visitor. It's that nice Scott Lavin."

The Hardys hurried downstairs and saw Scott standing in the doorway.

"You've got a lot of nerve coming here," Joe growled. "What do you want?"

Scott was holding something in his hands. He tossed it at Frank, who caught it reflexively. "I want you guys to help me find out what that thing is," Scott said.

Frank turned the metal object over in his hands, shrugged, and handed it to his brother. "Where did it come from?" Frank asked casually.

"I got it off McCoy's car at the bottom of the ocean," Scott admitted.

"You almost killed me for this thing!" Joe rasped, advancing on his friend.

Scott studied Joe with a look of disbelief. Then his eyes widened as the puzzled expression changed to one of shocked surprise. "You mean that was *you* down there?" he exclaimed.

He shook his head. "All I knew was that someone jumped me while I was trying to get back in my boat," he continued. "I was just trying to get away. I'm sorry, Joe. I didn't know!"

Frank quickly stepped between them and put his hand on his brother's tensed arm. "Why don't we go into the living room and talk about this some more?" he suggested calmly.

"I never trusted Arno," Scott explained, as they all sat down. "After the two 'accidents' that took me out of the race, I wanted to find out if McCoy's crash was fixed, too.

"So I took a dive down to the wreck and found that thing attached to the steering column," Scott continued, gesturing to the device in Joe's hands. "I know almost everything there is to know about Formula One design—and if that's a legit part of McCoy's steering system, I'll eat my car."

"Well, at least it's already been cooked," Joe joked halfheartedly.

"The steering system," Frank repeated. "That's it!"

Scott gave Joe a confused look. "What's he talking about?"

"Joe," Frank began, "remember what Phil said about the electronic device we found at the crash site?"

"Yeah," Joe nodded. "He said it was too complicated for a simple triggering device. It had to be part of something more complex."

"Right! Remote control steering! McCoy couldn't handle the car on the hairpin turn because someone else was steering by remote control!" Frank exclaimed, jumping up from his chair.

"But the remote operator would have to know exactly when the car got to the hairpin turn," he continued, pacing around the room as his mind unraveled the puzzle.

Joe could see where his brother's train of thought was going. "That means," he cut in, "it had to be someone who could *see* the car! And the only people who could see the car were—"

"The people in the helicopter." Frank finished the sentence with a smile. "Excluding you and me, that leaves the writer, the cameraman, the pilot, and—"

"Excuse me, boys," Gertrude interrupted, poking her head into the room. "But you have another visitor."

"Thank you, ma'am," a familiar voice came from behind her.

Russell Arno strode into the room, a coat draped over his right arm. "And now if you'll excuse us, the boys and I have some business to discuss."

Gertrude smiled. "Such a nice gentleman." She turned and walked out. "If you need anything," she called out, "I'll be in the kitchen."

"Oh, I think we have everything we need right here," Arno said coolly, pulling back the coat to reveal the automatic pistol in his hand that was aimed right at Joe.

"Don't we, boys?"

Chapter

13

ALL EYES IN the room were riveted on the gun.
"I think you have something that belongs to me,"
Arno said.

Joe started to stand up. "I told you what I'd
do if I caught you waving that thing around
again!" he snarled.

Frank reached out, put his hand on Joe's shoulder, and said, "Sit down, Joe. If the man wants
something so badly, let's give it to him."

Joe glanced at Frank and caught the slight wink
in his brother's eye. He felt the weight of the
object in his hand and turned back to the promoter. "Sure thing," he said, and smiled.
"Here—catch!"

Joe hurled the device at Arno's head as Frank
surged out of his seat, making a tackling dive for
the man's legs. Arno managed to dodge the chunk

of metal whizzing past his head, but the diversion was good enough.

Frank hurtled into him, hitting him just above the knees and knocking his legs out from under him. Arno crashed to the floor, the gun still clutched in his hand. Joe hesitated for a fraction of a second and then leaped for the arm holding the weapon. The promoter swung wildly, and a lucky blow cracked Joe on the head, the butt of the pistol slamming into his temple.

Joe fell back, dazed, pain shooting across his eyes. Everything went dark for a moment. He shook his head hard. Don't black out, he commanded himself. There's too much riding on this. He opened his eyes—and didn't like what he saw.

Arno was still on the floor, Frank's body sprawled across his legs, pinning him down. His hands were free, and in the right one he still clutched the gun. Now the barrel was pressed against the side of Frank's head.

"Move *very* slowly," Arno instructed. "Or your brother will have a very big hole in his head."

Joe staggered to his feet. "Look, you can have the thing," he said, pointing to the metal object lying on the floor. "Take it and get out. Just leave my brother alone."

Arno's gaze shifted to include Scott. "Hands on your head," he ordered the race car driver. "Bring that here," he said coldly to Joe, indicating the device. "But this time, *hand* it to me."

Joe picked it up and walked toward him. "That's close enough," Arno warned, reaching out with his free hand. "Now get your brother off me."

"I'm all right," Frank protested. "I can get up by myself."

"I'm sure you can," the promoter said. "But I want everybody's hands where I can see them—and I want them occupied."

Arno swung the gun around to include all three boys.

"Very good. Now I want you," he continued, poking Frank in the head with the gun barrel, "to clasp your hands behind your head. And I want you"—he nodded at Joe—"to pick him up. Scott, stay where you are."

Joe moved to help his brother up. "Not until I give the word!" Arno barked.

Joe froze. "Anything you say. You're the boss."

"That's better." Arno smiled. "Now, on the count of three. Ready? One—two—three."

Joe stooped down and took hold of Frank's arms near the shoulders. He grasped his brother firmly and pulled him to his feet. Joe gave Frank an apologetic look, and Frank just shrugged his shoulders. Things happen, the gesture said.

The promoter stood up, holding the gun in one hand and the device from the race car in the other hand. "Sit down, gentlemen," he ordered. "Now let's pretend I don't know what this is." He tapped the device lightly with the pistol. "And you're going to tell me all about it."

"If you don't know what it is," Frank said as he eased back into his chair, "why are you here, waving a gun in our faces?"

"I made the error of playing twenty questions with your brother," Arno began. "I won't make that mistake again. I'll hold the gun—you'll do the talking. Got it?"

A puzzled expression passed over Frank's face. "Okay. We'll play it your way," he said. "We got it off McCoy's car."

"Cute trick," Arno responded, "considering the fact that McCoy's car is at the bottom of the ocean. Try again."

"No, really," Scott Lavin interjected. "He's telling you the truth. We found that device attached to the steering column. The crash was no accident. That thing made it happen."

Joe shot Scott a look. Shut up, his eyes shouted, before you dig our graves any deeper!

Frank made a desperate attempt to gloss it over. "That's just a theory," he cut in. "What do we know? Right? A couple kids and a frustrated driver with a lump of charcoal for a car. We can't prove anything."

"No, no," Arno countered. "I think that's an excellent theory. You're probably right on track. Excellent work. I never would have thought of that. But you don't mind if I hold on to this for a few days, do you?"

"You mean you'll give it back?" Joe asked doubtfully.

"Look," Arno replied, his words dripping with impatience, "I didn't have anything to do with McCoy's death but I can't have a murder investigation delaying this race. This may sound cold-hearted to you, but time is money—and I'm only in it for the money."

"So what do you want from us?" Frank asked.

"The videotape your brother stole from my office," Arno said. "I didn't realize it was gone until this morning."

"Why didn't you just call the police?" Joe prodded.

"More questions," Arno snapped. "Just give me the tape and I'll be on my way."

"Aren't you worried that we might have watched it already?" Frank asked.

"There's really not much to see," Arno said. "Besides, it's a professional tape. Wrong format for a home VCR. Now, where is it? I'm getting impatient."

"It's not here!" Joe blurted out. "It's in a safe place."

"Oh, I see." Arno smiled thinly. "So the girl has it." He motioned to the door with the gun. "Come on. We're all going for a little ride."

Arno took his coat and draped it over his arm again, concealing the pistol in his hand. As the four of them headed for the front door they were intercepted by Aunt Gertrude. "Leaving so soon?'' she said. ''I was just coming to ask if you'd like some coffee or something.''

''Why, thank you, ma'am,'' Arno said, oozing with charm. ''But we really must be going now.''

''Oh?'' Gertrude responded, raising her eyebrows. ''It's getting awfully late, boys. Do you really think it's a good idea to go out now?''

''Under the circumstances,'' Frank said, shifting his gaze from his aunt to the coat slung over the promoter's arm, ''I think it's a very good idea.''

Joe saw what his brother was trying to do. ''A *very* good idea,'' he repeated forcefully, his eyes rapidly darting between his aunt and the concealed weapon.

''We'll only be at Callie's house, anyway,'' Frank added. ''You know where to find us.''

''Well, then I guess it's all right,'' Gertrude conceded. ''Have a nice time—and don't stay out too late.''

''I'll see that they're home by a reasonable hour,'' Arno assured her as he hustled the Hardys and Scott Lavin out into the yard, prodding Joe with the barrel of the gun.

Frank saw two cars parked in front. One, he knew, belonged to Scott. The other, he reasoned, must be Arno's. It was a two-seater sports car.

''Oh, too bad! Your car's not big enough for all of us,'' Frank said with mock disappointment. ''How about if we take the van and you follow us?''

115

"Yeah, great idea!" Joe chimed in. "We'll go real slow so you don't get lost."

"Let's all go together," Arno replied, shoving them toward the van.

"I'll drive," Frank stated flatly, heading for the left front door.

"Not so fast!" Arno retorted. Frank's hand was already on the handle. "You and Scott get in back with me," he said, nodding to Frank. "And you," he ordered, poking Joe in the back with the pistol, "drive."

They all climbed into the van, and Joe got behind the wheel. He started the engine, released the emergency brake, and rolled the van down the driveway toward the street. He knew his brother was up to something. He could tell by his tone of voice when he volunteered to drive. Frank's got some kind of plan, he told himself. I just wish I knew what it was!

Frank sat cross-legged on the floor of the van, his gaze never leaving Arno, sizing up the nervous promoter. There was no way he was going to let Arno get his hands on Callie. But it was going to be close, because he didn't want to take any chances in the van. If he tried to take Arno out while they were still moving and something went wrong, they could all be killed. Just have to wait until we get to Callie's house, he told himself, and hope Joe gets my signal.

Finally Joe pulled the van over to the curb and

shut off the engine. "Here we are," he said reluctantly as he set the emergency brake.

"You get out first," Arno instructed Joe. "Then come around and open the back door."

Joe hesitated. He glanced at his brother and saw that glimmer of a wink again. "Go ahead," Frank said. "Do what he says."

Joe started to open the door. "And don't forget the emergency brake," Frank added casually.

Joe stifled a smile as he got out of the van, quietly reaching down and releasing the brake with a smooth motion, unseen by Arno. "Right," he replied. "Almost forgot."

Frank couldn't tell for sure, but he thought Joe had gotten the message. Shifting his attention back to Arno, he waited for his brother to walk around to the back of the van. He had to make sure the promoter was the last one out.

As Joe swung the back door open, Frank said, "After you, Mr. Arno."

Arno shot him a suspicious look, and then smiled. "I'm calling the shots—if you'll pardon the expression—and I think you and Scott should get out first. That way all three of you will be in front of me, where I can see you."

Scott hopped out of the van, and Frank followed. He looked at his brother, and they shared a brief glance.

"Make sure your hands are where I can see them!" Arno barked as he started to climb out.

"Yes, sir!" Joe replied. "They're right here on the door!"

"Not your hands!" Arno snapped. "*His* han—"

While Joe distracted the promoter, Frank suddenly whirled around and lunged under Arno, shoving the bumper with both outstretched hands. The van lurched forward, and Arno pitched out headfirst.

This time, Joe didn't wait for him to hit the ground. He jumped out and drove his shoulder deep into the falling man's stomach.

"*Woof!*" Arno grunted as the wind was knocked out of him and the gun flew out of his hand. But Joe had hit him too low. Their combined momentum flipped Arno over Joe's back, and he landed right next to the weapon.

Arno snatched it up and scrambled to his feet. "Nobody move!" he screamed. "Or I start shooting!"

Frank picked himself up off the ground and advanced on the man. "You're not going to shoot anybody," he said calmly. "You've had plenty of chances, and you haven't fired a single shot. Give me the gun before somebody gets hurt."

As Frank reached out to take the weapon, Arno raised it high and swung down at him.

Frank threw his arms in the air, crossing them at the forearms to form an X over his head. He easily deflected the blow and trapped Arno's gun-wielding hand between his crossed arms. Then he twisted his body toward the promoter and grabbed hold of him at the wrist and just above the elbow. With a single, fluid motion, Frank flung Arno over his shoulder and onto the pavement.

Frank grasped Arno's wrist with both hands, making sure the gun wasn't pointed at anyone, and quickly moved in to put his foot in the promoter's armpit. "One hard tug," Frank said roughly, "and I'll dislocate your shoulder. I hear it hurts a lot."

Arno didn't say anything—but his hand went limp, and the weapon clattered harmlessly on the street.

"Now get up," Frank ordered. "You've got a lot of explaining to do."

Arno staggered to his feet. "You're right," he gasped.

Suddenly a shot rang out. Scott whirled in the direction of the sound, and Joe and Frank instinctively dove for cover.

Frank looked up and watched as Arno clutched at his chest, grimacing with pain. Then the promoter crumpled to the ground, blood seeping between his fingers and staining his shirt in a large circle.

Chapter

14

FRANK AND JOE lay flat on the ground. Out of the corner of his eye, Frank could see Scott Lavin crouching behind the van. "Stay where you are!" Frank hissed in a loud whisper. Scott probably wasn't going to move an inch until they pried him off the side of the van with a crowbar, but Frank wanted to make sure everything was under control before he made a move.

Frank turned his head toward Joe, who was lying next to him. "I'm going to see if I can drag Arno out of the line of fire." He started to squirm along the ground to where Arno lay motionless. A loud *crack* split the air, then a bullet *thunked* into the pavement, inches from Frank's head. A shard of concrete shrapnel sliced across his cheek, and he flattened and froze.

Pinned down—perfect, Frank thought. He

glanced at the promoter again. From the slowly spreading stain on his shirt, Frank could tell that the bullet had hit him in the shoulder.

"Mr. Arno!" he called out huskily. "Can you hear me?"

"Oooooh," came a low moan in reply.

Frank wasn't sure if he had really heard it or just imagined it.

Then it came again, louder this time. *Aaaooooh!*

It was a police siren—and it was getting close!

Frank heard footsteps running away, a door slamming, and a car engine starting.

Frank and Joe leapt up at the same time. "There he is!" Joe shouted, pointing down the street.

Frank caught a glimpse of the car as it squealed around the corner and out of sight. It was a Lotus sports coupe. And although it was too dark to make out the color, Frank was willing to bet it was silver gray.

The pulsing red and blue lights of a police cruiser came into view. The wail of the siren got painfully loud, and then abruptly stopped as the squad car pulled up to the curb.

"That was an awfully fast response," Joe commented, shielding his eyes from the flashing lights as the silhouette of a uniformed figure approached them.

"Not that we're complaining, mind you," Frank added. "But who called in the shooting?"

"What shooting?" came the tired voice of Con Riley. "Your aunt phoned the station and said you boys had been kidnapped by some guy with a gun hidden under his coat! Said he was going to nab Callie Shaw next."

The two brothers looked at each other and smiled. Aunt Gertrude had come through in the clutch.

"So where's this dangerous criminal?" Riley asked impatiently.

The smile faded from Frank's lips. "You'd better call an ambulance," he began, taking hold of Riley's arm and guiding him over to the injured promoter. "And you better put out an APB on a silver gray Lotus sports coupe."

The Hardys sat on Callie's front steps, under the eerie yellow glow of the porch light, and filled her in on the evening's events. They idly watched the police forensic team dig out the bullet that had kissed the pavement a hairbreadth from Frank's head. The lights were on in most of the neighbors' houses, and a throng of people in bathrobes, pajamas, and fuzzy slippers were milling around on the sidewalk.

"Most excitement they've had in years," Callie said.

"It's like some weird, late-night costume party," Joe muttered.

They could see that Scott Lavin had just finished giving his statement to one of the police officers. As the last of the police cars finally pulled away, he loped across the street to join the threesome. Callie turned to Frank and said, "So now you know Scott wasn't behind all this."

Frank nodded. "And Arno knows something, but he's not talking."

"Do you think that bullet he took was meant for us?" Joe asked.

Frank looked at his brother. "It fits the pattern. Before, they were just trying to scare us. Now they're playing for keeps."

"Now all you have to do is figure out who *they* are," Callie said.

Frank stood up. "Arno claimed there wasn't much to see on the videotape. But why would he go to so much trouble to get it back if there wasn't some crucial evidence in there somewhere?"

"Maybe we should take another look at it then," Joe suggested. "And maybe Scott can see something that we couldn't."

Frank grinned. "You read my mind, brother."

It was almost dawn when they replayed the tape for what seemed like the bazillionth time. "I'm sorry I can't help," Scott finally said. "But we already know *what* caused the crash. I can't see anything here that will tell us *who* caused it."

"And I don't see why we have to look at those stupid time codes ticking away at the bottom of the screen," Joe complained. "Isn't there any way to get rid of them?"

"They're permanently encoded on the master tape," Callie explained. "But I can set the machine so the time codes don't appear on the screen."

"That's it!" Frank shouted, jumping out of his chair. "The time codes!" He stepped quickly over to the video cassette machine. Frank had been watching Callie operate the thing for a couple of hours, and he practically had it memorized.

He hit a button on the console and the tape started to play from the beginning. "Not again!" his brother groaned.

Frank hit another button, and the scenes rushed by at a blurring rate. "What are you doing?" Callie asked.

"I'm going to cue up the scene where McCoy enters the tunnel," Frank said. "Right . . . here!" He pressed a third button, and the car froze on the screen, the cone-shaped nose just edging into the dark mouth of the tunnel. The digital clock at the bottom of the screen stopped, too. The time code was frozen at 00:09:33:18.

"Somebody write down the time," Frank ordered.

"I've got it," Callie said, taking a clipboard and a ballpoint pen from one of the shelves. "That's nine minutes, thirty-three seconds, and eighteen hundredths."

"Good," Frank said. He pressed the play button and the car started moving again. When the tape reached the point where the car started to emerge from the other end of the tunnel, he hit the freeze-frame again. Now the time code was 00:10:32:52.

"That's ten minutes, thirty-two seconds, and fifty-two hundredths," Callie read off the numbers as she wrote them down.

Scott Lavin frowned. "That's almost a full minute," he said.

"Doesn't seem very long to me," Joe responded. "It's a long tunnel."

"Not when you're going two hundred miles an hour," Frank pointed out. "How long do you think it would take, Scott?"

"Lap time is real important in racing," Scott explained. "So we keep track of time constantly. We know how long it should take us to get through each leg of the course. On my qualifying lap, I took that tunnel in about forty-four seconds. McCoy took fifteen seconds longer," he continued. "For a racing driver, that's forever."

"Long enough to stop and get out of the car?" Frank pressed.

"I guess," Scott said. "But why would he want to?"

Suddenly the answer dawned on Joe, and he was on his feet, pointing at the scene on the television. "So he wouldn't be *in* it when it went over the cliff!" he exclaimed.

"Then who was driving?" Callie wanted to know.

"McCoy," Frank answered.

"But you just said he wasn't in the car when it crashed," she countered.

"He wasn't," Joe agreed. "He was driving by remote control!"

"He faked his own death!" Frank laughed. "He's had us all running in circles!"

"Great theory, guys," Callie said, turning off the television and settling back down in her chair. "But what's his motive?"

"I heard he had some big debts," Scott offered. "Race cars are an expensive habit. McCoy's career was just beginning a downhill slide. He was losing sponsors. Maybe he did it for the insurance."

"I don't think so," Frank murmured. Something had just occurred to him, a conversation he'd had with someone. " 'This is the kind of ending publishers dream about,' " he mumbled. " 'The Fast Life and Tragic Death of Angus McCoy'."

He looked up and saw the others were staring at him. "Run that by me again," Joe said, furrowing his brow.

"It was something that writer, T. B. Martin, said," Frank explained. "Remember, Joe?"

Joe nodded. "That's right. He said McCoy's death would make a great ending for the book they were writing together. So maybe McCoy faked his own death to—"

"Turn an unsellable biography into the best-selling story of a racing legend's tragic and untimely death?" Frank finished the thought.

"But how would he collect his profits from the book sales?" Callie asked sleepily.

The sun's early rays were slanting in through the small windows set high in the basement walls, near the ceiling. Frank stifled a yawn. "Martin told me McCoy's royalties would go to a company called Clarco Industries. Maybe he can fill us in on the details."

"Does anybody know where to find him?" Scott asked.

Joe squinted through a shaft of light that had fallen across his face as the sun steadily rose in the sky outside. "Right now, he's probably having breakfast," he said. "But I know where he'll be in a couple of hours."

"Where's that?" Frank wanted to know.

"At the starting line of the Bayport Grand Prix," Joe said. "It's race day."

Chapter

15

"IT'S A BEAUTIFUL DAY for a race," Scott said softly as they walked out into the morning sun.

Joe looked at the sad expression on his friend's face. "I'm sorry about your car, Scott. If only we could have—"

"It wasn't your fault," Scott said, cutting him off. "In fact, you may have saved my life. Who knows what would have happened if I was out on the back stretch of the course doing a hundred eighty or a hundred ninety when that engine fire started."

Frank held open the van door while Scott and Callie climbed in. "Maybe it *is* our fault," Frank said.

"What do you mean?" Scott asked.

"The sabotage to your car was an afterthought. McCoy wanted us to think that somebody was trying to win the race by taking out all the front-runners. But if we hadn't pushed the investigation in the first place, he wouldn't have had to go to all the trouble.''

"That's right," Joe agreed, settling in behind the wheel. "The police were more than ready to believe McCoy's crash was an accident. McCoy was afraid that sooner or later we'd stop asking the *wrong* questions and start asking the *right* ones.''

Joe started the engine, checked the side mirrors, and put the van in gear. "Do you want me to drop you off someplace, Scott?" he asked.

Scott smiled weakly. "No, that's all right. I think I'll just tag along. Even if I'm not in the race, I have to see it. It's in my blood.''

Traffic was much heavier than usual. Bayport was crammed with vehicles, all headed in the same direction as the Hardys' van. The pace soon slowed to an agonizing stop-and-go crawl.

Frank gazed out the window and chuckled. "People from all over pile into their cars to go two miles an hour, so they can go watch somebody else drive two *hundred* miles an hour. Unbelievable.''

Finally they reached a police barricade. It was just a wood two-by-four that slanted down from a simple A-frame and rested on the pavement. On the side of the wood beam was stenciled: Police Line—Do Not Cross. It would be easy to move it out of the way—but the police officer guarding it made sure that no one did.

On the other side was the street that passed right through the middle of downtown Bayport. Scott showed his racing pass to the officer guarding the barricade, and the man picked up the end of the beam and swung it aside to let the van through.

In a few hours the street they were on would be full of screaming race cars, but for now they had it all to themselves. It was clear sailing until they got near the fairgrounds. There they ran into another kind of traffic jam—pedestrians.

Joe maneuvered the van slowly through the bustling congestion of mechanics, drivers, and race cars dotting the fairgrounds. They eventually worked their way to the shed that housed what was left of the McCoy Racing team and parked next to it. As they got out, Joe looked over at his brother. "Where's Callie?" he asked.

"She fell asleep in the back," Frank replied. "I didn't have the heart to wake her."

Reinhart Voss was in the shed, crawling around the huge rear wheels of his car, peering underneath the chassis, making his final inspection for the race. He saw Scott and got up, dusting off his knees and wiping off his hands. "I am glad you are here, Scott," he said. "There is something I would like to talk to you about."

"Before you get started," Frank interrupted.

"We're looking for the writer, T. B. Martin. Have you seen him?"

"Yes." Voss nodded. "He was here, but he forgot his tape recorder and went back to the motel to get it."

"Then that's where we're going," Frank said.

"Catch you later!" Joe called back to Scott as he hurried off after his brother.

The Hardys threaded their way back to the Bayport Motel and headed for the front desk. Frank approached the clerk behind the counter and smiled. "I'm T. B. Martin. Could I have my room key, please?"

The clerk turned to a honeycomb of cubby holes on the wall, each with a number below it. He reached for one and then turned back to Frank, empty-handed. "Your key isn't in your slot," he said with a frown. "Could I see some kind of identification?"

"Sure thing," Frank agreed cheerfully, reaching into his right back pocket. His smile faded as he tried his other back pocket. "Uh-oh. I must've left my wallet in the car. I'll be right back."

Frank and Joe turned around and headed back in the direction of the front door. When they were sure the desk clerk wasn't watching, they swerved over to the elevators.

"Eighth floor," Frank said, stepping into the elevator after his brother.

"Right," Joe replied, running his finger down

the bank of numbers and pressing one of the recessed buttons. A tiny light winked on to indicate the one he had touched. "The clerk reached for the slot marked eight-thirteen. That must be Martin's room."

The light inside the button marked 8 winked off as the elevator door slid open and the Hardys got off. "Wouldn't it have been easier to just call him from the lobby?" Joe asked as they walked down the hall.

"That would spoil the surprise," Frank said.

They passed Room 811 on the left and Room 812 on the right. At the next door on the left, Frank stopped and raised his hand to knock. But the door swung open before he could complete the motion.

T. B. Martin strode out, clutching a small portable tape recorder in one hand. "Well, if it isn't the Hardy brothers," he said. "I hope you guys weren't coming to see me. I'm in kind of a hurry."

He closed the door to his room and brushed past the Hardys, walking toward the elevator. Then he paused, turned around, and looked at Frank. "You know," he said, "I was just thinking about you. Well, not so much you personally, but something you asked me about the other day."

Frank raised an eyebrow. "Oh? And what might that be?"

"You were asking me about McCoy's share of

the profits on his book," Martin replied. "I told you about the contract and Clarco Industries."

"Right," Frank nodded. "I remember."

"Well, I just got a registered letter this morning from the Clarco offices. It appears the company has gone belly-up—bankrupt—and the book contract was bought by some guy named Jason Drake."

"Do you have any idea who this Drake character is?" Joe asked.

Martin shook his head. "None whatsoever. So now I've got a silent, invisible partner." He paused as a large grin spread across his face. "With any luck, he'll *stay* that way, and I can write this biography *my* way.

"Are you guys going to the race?" he asked as he turned to walk down the hall.

"Not right now," Frank responded, nudging Joe and following the writer. "But we'll ride down in the elevator with you."

"Okay," Martin said as they descended to the lobby. "But don't forget you still owe me an interview."

The Hardys watched Martin leave the hotel and head off in the direction of the fairgrounds. Then they strolled back into the lobby and found a couple of empty chairs.

"What now?" Joe asked, slouching down in a seat facing his brother. "We know the name McCoy is using—but we don't know where to find him."

Frank closed his eyes, lost in thought.

"McCoy must have gone to a lot of trouble to set up a new identity," Frank finally said after a long pause. "And we know he was still in town a couple of hours ago."

"Right," Joe agreed. "He took a couple whacks at us with a high-powered rifle and hit Arno by mistake."

"He probably has some kind of disguise," Frank continued, "but he still wouldn't want to be seen in public too much. So he'd need a place to stay."

"Well, we're sitting in the lobby of the nearest place to do that," Joe observed.

"Exactly," Frank said with a grin.

Joe sat up straight in his seat. "You mean you think he's *here?*"

"There's an easy way to find out," Frank replied.

He got up and walked over to the front desk. Joe was right behind him. "Excuse me," Frank addressed the desk clerk. "Could you tell me if you have a Jason Drake registered at the hotel?"

The man behind the counter squinted suspiciously at Frank. "Haven't I seen you before?"

"Not likely," Joe cut in. "We just flew in from Pocatello, Idaho. Ever been to Pocatello?"

"Ahhh—no," the clerk replied in a flustered tone. "I'm sorry, I must have been mistaken." He looked down at his computer console and started typing on the keyboard. "Let's see—Mr.

Drake checked out. In fact, I just sent a bellhop up to his room to help him carry down his bags.''

"And what room might that be?" Frank asked, leaning across the counter and craning his neck to get a look at the computer screen.

"Now I remember you!" the clerk exclaimed. You were here a little while ago. You told me you were—"

"Got to go!" Joe interrupted, grabbing Frank's arm and hauling him away from the counter. "Don't want to miss our flight back to Idaho!"

They turned and walked quickly out the front door, leaving the desk clerk spluttering to himself.

"How do we find Drake now?" Joe asked. "Follow everybody who leaves the hotel?"

"We don't have to find him," Frank replied. "He's going to find us."

Joe glanced at his brother. "And where is he going to find us?"

"Over there," Frank said, pointing to the motel parking garage.

It wasn't hard to find the silver gray Lotus. Joe and Frank spotted it right away. They crouched behind the car next to it and waited.

"How do we know he won't have the parking attendant drive it around to the front entrance?" Joe asked.

"When you own a car like that," Frank said, "you don't let anybody else even touch it."

"The guy goes to a lot of trouble to conceal his identity," Joe whispered, "and then he drives around in a flashy sports car."

Frank shrugged. "Old habits die hard."

They heard footsteps echoing through the garage, moving in their direction. Frank put his index finger to his lips, and Joe nodded. The footsteps grew louder and then stopped nearby. There was a jingle of keys and the sound of a car door being unlocked. Frank got down on his hands and knees and peered under the car. All he could see was a pair of expensive leather boots against the open door of the silver gray sports car.

Frank signaled to Joe, and they both circled around the car from opposite sides, trapping the man between them.

Frank smiled. "Angus McCoy, I presume."

Chapter

16

THE MAN STANDING next to the sports car froze, his back to Frank. "You've made some kind of mistake," he said with a slight British accent. "My name is Drake."

"It is *now*," Frank agreed, closing the distance between them. "But a couple days ago it was—"

Suddenly the man spun around, swinging a heavy suitcase in his outstretched right hand, and cracked Frank square on the jaw. The blow knocked Frank backward, and he sprawled across the trunk of the car behind him.

"That's the last cheap shot you take at us!" Joe growled, coming at the man from the other side. He got a good look at "Drake." Joe guessed that he was about the same size as McCoy, although the cowboy hat perched on his head made him look a little taller. The wide brim of the hat made it hard to see the man's hair and eyes, but it was McCoy.

"Come on," Joe said sharply, shifting his weight on his feet and gesturing with his right hand. "Just you and me now, one on one. I can take you."

The man looked at Joe, sizing him up. Then he shrugged his shoulders and smiled. "You probably could," he agreed, and bolted for the garage entrance.

Joe ran over to his brother and helped him to his feet. "Are you okay?"

"I've been better," Frank muttered, rubbing his jaw. "But don't stop on account of me—let's get after him!"

The Hardys ran out of the garage and looked up and down the street. "There he goes!" Joe yelled, pointing off in the distance. "He's headed for the fairgrounds!"

They charged after him, running side by side. "Can't let him get too far ahead," Frank said, huffing, "or we'll lose him in the crowd."

"I don't think that's going to be a problem," Joe replied, watching the cowboy hat bobbing and weaving through the throng of racing personnel and curious spectators. He saw the hat veer off to the right and caught a glimpse of the man as he darted into one of the nearby sheds.

There was some muffled shouting and then the earsplitting roar of a Formula One engine. A race car lurched out of the shed, with a couple of very angry men in pursuit. One of them was obviously the guy who was *supposed* to be in the car, Joe noted, because he was wearing a one-piece protective driving suit.

The sleek, low-slung racing machine swerved out onto the roadway and took off down the course. "That's him!" Joe shouted. "He just stole that car!" Then he looked at his brother and said, "Well, two can play that game."

"What do you mean?" Frank asked. But Joe had already surged ahead through the crowd.

Joe ran straight for the McCoy Racing shed. He skidded to a stop out in front and peered inside. Scott Lavin and Reinhart Voss were absorbed in conversation. The mechanic was putting the last of his tools away. Joe took a deep breath and walked calmly up to the race car. He swung his right leg over the side, then his left, and sat down on something hard and uncomfortable. It was Voss's crash helmet. Joe quietly fished it out from under him and slid the rest of the way into the cockpit. Then he pulled on the helmet and strapped himself in.

Joe held his breath and reached for the starter switch. *Lucky these babies don't need keys,* Joe thought, a brief smile passing over his lips. *Otherwise I'd look pretty stupid sitting here.*

He flipped the switch and was rewarded with the deafening blast of the 900-horsepower engine behind him bursting into life, the painful sound reverberating off the aluminum walls of the shed.

Frank arrived just in time to see the race car squeal out of the shed and onto the road. The sight of Reinhart Voss and Scott Lavin staring in amazement only confirmed what Frank already knew.

He didn't waste any time. He hurried over to Voss and said, "There's a two-way radio in that thing, isn't there?"

Voss just gave him a glazed look.

"We can *talk* to him, can't we?" Frank prodded.

"Oh, yes. Sure," Voss said after a moment. "We have a whole control center here, with a radio to communicate with the car anytime."

"Then let me talk to him," Frank urged.

The other driver had about a thirty-second lead on Joe, but he was hampered by scattered pedestrians on the course. The race wasn't scheduled to start for another hour, and people were still milling around, sometimes darting across the roadway, looking for a better vantage point to view the race. The lead car had cleared the way for Joe, and he could see it ahead as he rocketed down a straightaway.

Joe was surprised at how bumpy the ride was. His head was buffeted from side to side, and he could feel every little flaw in the road. Then he remembered that the car was designed that way— the aerodynamic "ground effects" practically sucked the bottom of the car to the pavement for better handling.

No wonder racing drivers wear helmets, he thought as his head slammed into the back of the seat and then rocked forward again. It keeps them from getting punch drunk.

He was closing in on the other car when it dawned on him that he had no idea what he was going to do once he caught up with it. Suddenly he heard a tinny voice squawking in his ear. "Joe, are you there? Can you hear me?"

"Great," he said out loud. "Now I'm hearing voices. Maybe it's my conscience—but why does it sound like Frank?"

"Joe," the voice came again, "if you can hear me, hit the talk-back switch on the console."

Joe realized it was the cockpit radio and flipped the switch. "Hey, brother!" he shouted over the roar of the wind and the engine. "What's shaking?"

"Sounds like you are," Frank quipped over the speaker. "Listen, I've got a plan."

"I hope it's better than mine."

"All you have to do is keep him on the race course. He won't even try to get off until he's well away from the congested downtown area, and even then he'll have to stop the car, get out, and move a barricade out of the way."

"I'm with you so far," Joe replied, switching his right foot from the gas to the brake and cranking the wheel hard to the left for a tight turn. He felt the back tires start to slide, and he pulled the wheel back to the right. The race car fishtailed wildly as it came out of the turn, and Joe thought he was going to lose it.

"Whoa!" he yelled as he fought with the steering wheel.

"Joe!" Frank cried. "Are you all right?"

There was silence on the other end, and then, "Um—no problem. Everything's under control now. So you were saying?"

"All you have to do is stay close enough to prevent him from driving off the course onto some side road," Frank explained. "No heroics, okay?"

"Hey, you know me," Joe said.

"Yeah, that's what I'm afraid of," Frank replied. He handed the microphone to Scott Lavin and said, "Try to talk him through it."

"Where are you going?" Scott asked.

"I'm going to take a little drive myself," Frank said.

Frank hopped in the van, which was parked outside the shed, and started heading directly across the fairgrounds. The rough ride on the open terrain jostled Callie Shaw awake. She rubbed her eyes and said, "Where are we going?"

"McCoy stole a Formula One car and took off down the course, trying to escape. I don't have to tell you who's chasing him in Voss's car." Frank was silent for a moment, devoting his attention to a tight turn. Then he added, "I'm going to head them off."

Callie glanced at Frank. "In this thing? How will we even *catch* them, much less head them off?"

"Simple," Frank began. "The fairgrounds are in the northwest part of Bayport. The race course runs along the eastern border of the fairgrounds and then south through downtown. Then the course swings way out to the west and up the highway before turning back east to the ocean.

"We're taking a little shortcut to the north," he finished.

"But that will take us right out onto the cliff road!" Callie protested.

Frank nodded. "That's the idea."

"How are you holding up?" Scott's voice squawked in Joe's ear.

"I'm okay on the straightaways," Joe grumbled, "but he keeps moving farther ahead of me on every turn."

"What did you expect?" came the reply. "He's a pro. Just remember what I told you. Slow down before you hit the curve, and don't do a lot of down-shifting. Keep it in a high enough gear so you won't lose a lot of time shifting back up when you come out of the turn.

"Keep your hands at the ten and two o'clock positions on the wheel," Scott went on. "Cross your arms on the turns if you have to, but don't move your hands."

Joe's hands were gripping the wheel so tightly that they were turning white. "Right," he said. "I think I've got that one down pat. But I've got to close the distance somehow."

Joe saw the car ahead of him veer over to the side and slow down near a blocked-off cross street. "We'll have another driving lesson later!" he shouted. "It looks like he's making his move!"

He punched the accelerator to the floor and tore down the road, heading straight for the other race car. McCoy saw him coming, swerved back to the middle of the road and sped up again—but not fast enough. Now Joe was right on his tail, in his slipstream.

Joe eased off the accelerator slightly, letting the air currents in the wake of the lead car pull him along for the ride. "Got you now!" Joe yelled. "I'm hanging onto your tail, and I'm not letting go!"

The car in front careened from one side of the road to the other and back again, trying to shake Joe off. But Joe matched it move for move. They blasted up the long north straightaway, locked in an invisible embrace. Joe knew they must be doing close to 190, but the constant bumping and rocking, with his head just a few feet off the ground, made it feel as if they were about to break the speed of sound.

Still he felt oddly calm as the eastward uphill

turn loomed ahead. It was a right turn, and Joe was ready when the lead car moved to the left side of the road to reduce the angle of the curve and take it at the fastest speed possible.

Joe followed the maneuver easily, staying right behind him. Looking at the shadows cast by the late-morning sun, Joe couldn't tell where one car ended and the other began. The flared rear wing of one merged with the tapered nose of the other.

Then suddenly the car in front swerved back into the right lane and the driver downshifted, lurching to a reduced speed. Joe shot past him and realized, too late, that he was going way too fast to make the turn.

Joe slammed on the brakes, making another disastrous mistake. The nose dipped down and scraped the pavement. The rear end bucked up and the back tires lost their grip on the road, sliding sideways and throwing the car into a deadly spin.

Joe fought the wheel, but there was no response. The car was completely out of control.

Chapter

17

THE RACE CAR spun around violently and skidded backward onto the shoulder of the road. Any other vehicle would have flipped over, crushing the driver underneath. But the low center of gravity kept the Grand Prix racer upright.

Joe was rattled but unhurt. He pried his hands off the steering wheel. They were shaking badly. He willed himself to calm down, but he remembered to keep his foot on the gas pedal, keeping the revs high enough to prevent the engine from stalling out. He glanced at the array of gauges. Everything seemed okay. None of the needles were poking into the red zone.

All of this took a matter of seconds, although it seemed like an eternity to Joe. He was now pointing in the wrong direction, and he could see the other Formula One car in the side mirror, dwindling in the distance.

Joe eased off the clutch, the wheels kicking up gravel as the car moved off the side and back onto the pavement. Joe pulled the wheel hard to the left and made a tight U-turn, skirting the outer edge of the shoulder on the opposite side. Then he grimly pressed the accelerator to the floor, his head jerking backward as the car took off in pursuit.

Frank pulled the van out onto the cliff road about a half mile down from the hairpin turn. He glanced at his watch as he raced up the road. It had only been nine minutes since McCoy had fled the fairgrounds in the stolen car.

"What happens if they come zooming right down our throats?" Callie asked nervously.

Frank flashed a tight grin. "The van will end up with a very exotic hood ornament. But don't worry—we've still got at least a minute and a half."

Frank slowed down for the tight curve where McCoy's race car had crashed through the guardrail from the opposite direction just a few days ago. He steered the van onto the narrow shoulder at the edge of the cliff and then backed it up so that it was now blocking the road.

Frank leapt out of the van and Callie chased after him. "How do you know we have that much time?"

"Because of the time codes on the videotape," Frank reminded her. "It took McCoy ten minutes and thirty seconds to get to this end of the tunnel.

"Here, help me with this," he grunted, swinging the barricade with the flashing lights away from the gap in the guardrail, and blocking the outer shoulder of the road with it.

"But why here?" Callie pressed.

"Because this is the best place to stop him," Frank explained. "This hairpin turn is the trickiest part of the course. He'll be slowing down as he comes out of the tunnel, so he'll be able to stop safely when he sees the van blocking the road. There won't be enough room to turn around, and Joe will shut him in from the other end."

Frank looked at his watch again. He went to the back of the van and opened the rear door.

Callie rolled her eyes. "What now?"

"Still thirty seconds left," Frank said. "You get behind the van. I'm going to set out some emergency flares just to make sure he gets the idea."

He took out the flares and set one in the middle of the road, about twenty yards in front of the van. Then he ran back and knelt down next to the barricade on the shoulder, setting another flare in front of it.

Frank was about to stand up when he heard a rumbling noise behind him. He looked over his shoulder and saw a Formula One car come roaring out of the tunnel and screech to a halt near the first emergency flare.

Frank swore softly under his breath. Too late, he remembered the extra fifteen seconds it had taken McCoy to get out of his car on the day of the crash. And now he's caught me off guard, Frank realized. Right out in the open.

He couldn't make out the driver's identity—his face, from the nose down, was blocked by the lip of the cockpit. But Frank could see his steel gray eyes. They were locked on him, staring *through* him.

As Frank heard the powerful engine rev up, he knew that the man behind the wheel of the race car was going to try to smash through the wooden barrier and take the narrow outer shoulder around the van. He was willing to risk his life for his freedom—and he wouldn't hesitate to run Frank over if he was in the way.

The driver popped the clutch and the car jumped forward. Frank dove for the side of the van. He looked up to see the race car angling toward the barrier, still not going too fast. Then he heard a familiar rumbling sound. Another car was coming through the tunnel!

The second car slowed and came out of the tunnel to smash into the left rear side of the first one, twisting it sideways on the road. As the back end of the lead car swung around from the impact, the driver bashed his head on the side of the cockpit. The man inside slumped forward, and the engine sputtered and died.

The engine of the other race car revved to a high-pitched whine in triumph. Then it settled back down to a low rumble before the driver switched off the ignition. He climbed out, took off his crash helmet, and ran his hand through his blond hair.

It was Joe. He glanced inside the other car, and then he looked at his brother and smiled. "Looks like a TKO to me. Does that mean I win?"

They pulled Angus McCoy from the cockpit and laid him down gently next to the race car.

Frank reached into the car Joe had been driving and flipped the radio talk-back switch. "You better get an ambulance up here. It looks like the reports of Angus McCoy's death were greatly exaggerated."

A police cruiser escorted the ambulance to the scene. Officer Con Riley got out of the police car, followed by Scott Lavin and Reinhart Voss. "Looks like I was wrong about you boys after all," Riley scowled. "You *are* a couple of car thieves."

Joe shrugged. "I figured it was only fair to chase down McCoy in a car that belonged to him."

Voss looked over the Formula One machine. "There's no real damage," he concluded. "It's still in pretty good driving condition."

"What's all this about McCoy still being alive?" Riley demanded.

"See for yourself." Frank jerked his thumb over his shoulder.

A paramedic from the ambulance was helping a slightly shaken but unmistakable Angus McCoy to his feet. Joe winked. "Looks like the real McCoy to me."

"Well, I'll be!" Riley exclaimed, pushing his patrolman's hat back on his forehead.

"Before you take him away, we'd like to ask him a few questions," Frank said. "You don't mind, do you, Con?"

Riley frowned. "I don't even know what to charge him with. Impersonating a dead man?"

"Stick around," Joe said. "You might learn something."

McCoy seemed calm and relaxed, almost resigned. But his eyes still radiated a sense of confidence as they locked on Frank. "I should have known you were going to be trouble from the moment I saw you nosing around the crash site."

"You *saw* us?" Joe asked.

"Sure," Frank said. "He had to be hiding inside the tunnel, watching everything. He had to wait until we all left before he could make his getaway."

"Then what did he do?" Callie wanted to know. "*Walk* back to town?"

"Well, *part* of the way," Frank replied. "We

found footprints up on the ridge, but he probably had the Lotus hidden in the woods farther down the access road.

"He was going to leave town," Frank continued, "but he got nervous after he saw me pick up that piece of the remote control device. There's probably more evidence around here, too."

Frank turned to McCoy. "My guess is you loosened the bolts on the guardrail to make sure the car went over the edge. Right?"

McCoy shrugged. "You're doing just fine all by yourself. You don't need my help."

"You're right," Frank said. "I don't. McCoy started following us around. When Joe and I split up, he stuck with me since I was the one who found the device in the first place. He followed me to Phil Cohen's house and then back to Scott's garage."

"Right," Joe agreed. "Then he knocked Frank out and tried to make it look like an accident. When he realized Frank wasn't carrying the gizmo, he doubled back to Phil's place, sucker-punched Phil, grabbed the doohickey, and set the fire to cover his tracks."

McCoy frowned slightly. "I'm sorry about your friend. But you forced my hand."

"But that wasn't enough." Frank picked up the story. "McCoy wanted to wipe the slate clean. So he broke into Arno's office, looking for the videotape of the crash, but he couldn't find it. So he tried to throw us off the track again by sabotaging Scott's car, making it look like someone who wanted to win the race was behind the whole thing."

"And when *that* didn't work," Joe said, "McCoy decided to use us for target practice, but he hit Arno by mistake."

McCoy chuckled softly. "I don't hit people I'm not aiming at."

Frank and Joe exchanged a puzzled glance.

McCoy smiled thinly. "It looks like you boys don't know *everything*. Arno knew I was up to something. He found out about the Clarco Industries scam I was using to stash my money."

"The canceled checks!" Joe burst out.

McCoy nodded. "Sooner or later Arno would have figured out the whole thing."

"I think he may have caught on a lot quicker than you think," Joe said. "He took out a million-dollar life insurance policy on you!"

"It figures." McCoy sighed. "That two-bit hustler was always trying to cash in on my sweat and blood."

Frank looked at the world champion driver. "You seem to be taking all this pretty well."

McCoy shrugged. "A race car has ten thousand parts. Even if it's 99.9% perfect, there are still ten things that can go wrong. But there's no sense getting mad at the car. My plan wasn't perfect. You won. I lost. No hard feelings."

Con Riley slapped a pair of handcuffs on McCoy and led him away. Joe turned to Scott Lavin and said, "I'm sorry about the way things worked out. This should have been your big day, but now you don't even have a car."

"Oh, but I do!" Scott smiled. He patted Reinhart Voss on the back. "Reinhart made me an offer I couldn't refuse."

"It is nothing, really," the German driver said. "I told Scott he could drive my car. As I said before, this race is not that important for me. But for Scott it could mean much. So I said to myself, why not? And with Angus gone, who is there to say no?

"What could be more simple?" Voss went on. "Until you came along and took off in my race car like some crazy person! Lucky for you, the car is all right, and Scott will have his chance after all."

"You mean, after all this, there's still going to be a race?" Callie asked in disbelief.

Joe grinned from ear to ear and clapped Frank on the shoulder. "A Grand Prix race is like the Hardy brothers—*nothing* stops us!"

Frank and Joe's next case:

When the Hardys visit a local movie and TV studio they stumble across a real-life drama— someone has murdered screenwriter Bennett Fairburn. To track the killer the brother detectives go undercover as gofers at the studio.

From the start it's clear that Frank and Joe have been cast as victims in a sinister plot. A series of deadly "accidents" stalk the brother team, and while shooting a TV series they find themselves on the wrong end of some lethal stunts. The clues they need are buried in the script, but unless they uncover the villain fast, the brothers Hardy will be show biz history . . . in *Final Cut,* Case #34 in The Hardy Boys Casefiles™.